TALES FROM
THE
CARIBBEAN

TRISH COOKE was born in Bradford, West Yorkshire. Her parents are from Dominica in the West Indies, and she comes from a big family with six sisters and three brothers. For eight years, Trish was presenter and scriptwriter on the hit preschool BBC programme *Playdays* and has many other acting credits. She also writes scripts for TV, theatre and radio. Trish has written stories for as long as she can remember. Visit her at www.trishcooke.co.uk.

TRISH COOKE

TALES FROM

THE CARIBBEAN

Illustrations by JOE LILLINGTON

PUFFIN CLASSICS

PUFFIN BOOKS

UK | USA | Canada | Ireland | Australia
India | New Zealand | South Africa

Puffin Books is part of the Penguin Random House group of companies
whose addresses can be found at global.penguinrandomhouse.com.

www.penguin.co.uk
www.puffin.co.uk
www.ladybird.co.uk

First published 2017
001

Text copyright © Trish Cooke, 2017
Illustrations by Joe Lillington
Illustrations copyright © Penguin Books Ltd, 2017

The moral right of the author and illustrator has been asserted

Typeset in 11.5/15 pt by Minion
Typeset by Jouve (UK), Milton Keynes
Printed in Great Britain by Clays Ltd, St Ives plc

A CIP catalogue record for this book is available from the British Library

ISBN: 978-0-141-37308-9

All correspondence to
Puffin Books
Penguin Random House Children's
80 Strand, London WC2R 0RL

For my granddaughters,
Chantelle and Charmaine

Also in Puffin Classics

TALES FROM AFRICA
by K. P. Kojo

TALES FROM INDIA
by Bali Rai

and by Roger Lancelyn Green

TALES OF THE GREEK HEROES
MYTHS OF THE NORSEMEN
TALES OF ANCIENT EGYPT

Contents

AUTHOR'S NOTE

My mother and father travelled from the Caribbean to the UK in the late 1950s, as did so many other West Indians at that time. I was born in the UK, in Bradford, Yorkshire, and my parents are from the Commonwealth of Dominica. In Bradford, thousands of miles away from the tropical Caribbean island of Dominica, my parents told me stories about sookooyahs and Jab and characters like the mischievous Compère Lapin. They also told me about real people they remembered too, larger-than-life characters. Carnival songs have been made about some of them. At the time, I did not realize my parents were passing on a legacy. The precious stories they were sharing with me were a link to their past, my heritage, some of which were told to them by family members or *raconteurs*.

Long before TV and internet, people in Dominica would often share stories at outside gatherings. When the raconteur announced he was going to begin a story he would call to the people '*Eh Kwik!*' and the people would answer 'Eh Kwak!' and the raconteur would call again 'Eh Kwik!' and he would do so several times during the story, and each time he called the people listening would call back 'Eh Kwak!' This call and response traditional way of telling Caribbean folk tales has its roots in African storytelling. Different Caribbean islands have their own call and response phrases. I have used the Eh Kwik, Eh Kwak call and response style of storytelling in the retelling of 'The Man and his Servant', a folk tale from Dominica. Call and response works particularly well when read out loud with a group. For the rest of the stories I have used a traditional classic folk-tale style of telling, making the content of the stories (without the performing storyteller) the main focus. These stories can be shared or read alone.

The stories in this book have a mixture of West African and Amerindian roots. 'Two Dinners' is based on an Ashanti story brought over to the Caribbean from West Africa and features the familiar Brer Anansi, a popular character in Jamaican folklore. 'The First Kingfisher' and 'The Spirit of the Rock' have their roots in the traditions of Carib folklore and they each have a strong mythological element featuring spirits, rituals and spells based on the beliefs of the indigenous Carib people.

I have chosen to retell stories from the Commonwealth of Dominica, Guyana, Jamaica, Tobago, the Dominican Republic, Trinidad, St Vincent, St Lucia, Haiti, Martinique and Antigua. Each Caribbean island has its own stories.

It is also common to find versions of the same stories in different islands, with characters such as Anansi (Jamaica), Compère Lapin (Dominica, St Lucia) or Brer Rabbit playing the same trickster character in them all.

In my version of these Caribbean tales I have added and taken away some elements to tell the stories in my own way. This is quite common with Caribbean folk tales, as originally the stories were passed down by word of mouth and the storyteller would have added and taken away parts of the story to make it work for a specific audience. In their original oral form the stories would have been told using the colloquial language, patois or Kwéyòl of the specific island, but I have used mostly standard English. I have had such fun researching these stories and finding my own way of telling them.

Enjoy!

TC

The First Kingfisher

This story is based on a Carib (Callinago)
legend from the Commonwealth of Dominica

Long, long ago, when roads were not quite roads but just footpaths and tracks formed between trees and bushes (made by the many who walked from village to town), there was an island called *Why-took-abuli*. The shape of the island resembled that of a tall woman and the Callinago people who lived there had named it so, for *Why-took-abuli* means 'how tall is her body'. On this island there lived a grumpy little man called Karahu. Karahu had a frown always fixed on his face. His brow was always furrowed and his shoulders always hunched over. He lived in a small house on a plateau by a lake and

1

he spent his days fishing. Karahu would fish alone, cook alone, eat alone and sleep alone. He had no one to share his life with and he was very, very lonely.

All day long he would mumble and moan to himself, 'What a life . . . what a life . . . I wish I had company!' More than anything in the world, Karahu longed for someone to share his life with.

One day, Karahu was fishing by the lake as usual when he noticed a colourful stone by the water's edge. The stone glistened in the sunlight, radiating all the colours of the rainbow.

'I am your magic stone,' the stone whispered. 'What is it you most desire in the whole world?'

Karahu couldn't believe what he was hearing. Was he out of his mind? How could a stone be speaking to him? He thought perhaps the sound of the stone whispering was in fact the sound of ripples in the water, or the gentle breeze rustling the trees around him. Perhaps his mind was just playing tricks on him. So Karahu ignored the murmurings from the stone and carried on with his fishing.

Then the stone spoke again. 'I am your magic stone. What is it you most desire in the whole world?'

Karahu immediately stopped fishing and looked at the colourful stone in shock.

'In all my life I have never seen or heard such a thing!' he said. 'Are you truth or dream?'

'Truth,' whispered the colourful stone. 'And I haven't got all day! Answer me now before I change my mind.'

'In that case,' Karahu said quickly, 'that's easy. More than anything in the world, I would like a wife to share my life with.'

'So be it,' said the stone. 'I will grant your wish. Continue your life as before . . . your wife is on her way.'

Karahu was in shock. He didn't know what to do. He had never had a stone speak to him before and still he wasn't sure if it was just his mind playing tricks on him. But he didn't want to miss out on the opportunity of getting a wife to keep him company, so he did as the stone had told him. He continued to fish, went home, cooked, ate and slept as before. He even cleaned himself up, bathed and shaved so he would look good for when his wife arrived. And each day Karahu went back to the lake to fish, and he waited and waited for the wife the stone had promised him. But each day, all he came home with was the fish he had caught. He sat at home, alone, waiting for his wife. But there was no sign of her. After a week Karahu gave up on his foolish dream and he went back to his mumbling and moaning.

'What a life . . . what a life . . . I wish I had company!' And he forgot all about bathing and shaving and making himself presentable.

Not long after this, in a village a few miles away from Karahu's home, a Carib named Amos and his wife

Sylvan had to go to town for business. In those days the Caribs went everywhere on foot and it took days and days to get into town. Amos and Sylvan gathered their things together and arranged to travel with a few friends who also had to go to town. They rose bright and early and set off on the long journey. As they went along they sang and, as the custom was, they clapped their hands and slapped their thighs.

'Clap hands and slap our thighs,
Clap hands and slap our thighs,
Clap hands and slap our thighs,
We'll be on our way . . .'

They had brought enough food and drink to keep them going. The journey felt like a party.

After a little while Sylvan decided she wanted to take a rest from all the dancing, so she sat down by a lake with her feet in the water and told her husband, Amos, that she would catch them up. Amos and the others went along their way, singing and dancing as before.

'Clap hands and slap our thighs,
Clap hands and slap our thighs,
Clap hands and slap our thighs,
We'll be on our way . . .'

After Sylvan had rested for a little while, she stood and looked out across the lake. 'What a beautiful lake!' she said to herself. Looking down on the ground, Sylvan noticed the same colourful stone that Karahu had seen weeks ago. Once again, the stone was glistening in the sunlight, radiating all the colours of the rainbow.

What an unusual stone, Sylvan thought, and she picked it up and took it with her. She hurried to catch up with the others but she could not see them anywhere. She listened to see if she could hear them singing but she couldn't hear them either. 'That's strange,' she said to herself, 'I must have rested for longer than I thought. My husband and friends must be a long way ahead of me.' Sylvan began to walk more quickly to catch them up but, after a while, she found herself back by the lake where she had started. It was beginning to get dark.

What am I doing still here by the lakeside? Sylvan thought. Then, as she looked one way and then the other, she noticed a bright glow lighting her way. It was coming from the colourful stone in her hand. *How amazing!* she thought. *The stone is like a torch lighting my path. Maybe, if I follow it, it will lead me to the others.* Once again Sylvan set off on her journey, this time following the glow of light coming from the stone in her hand. She walked and walked but once again she only returned to where she had started. 'How can that be?' she said to herself. 'I've walked for such a long time and yet I am still by the lakeside!'

Tired and weary, Sylvan clasped the glowing stone in her hand and walked as fast as she could. But still she found herself back where she started. 'Oh no!' she sobbed as she threw the stone down. 'This is terrible! I'm lost! How am I to find my way out of here?'

Refusing to give up, she set off again. She walked and she walked, on and on, up and up, until finally she came to a plateau. She crossed the plateau and saw a little house ahead of her. *At last*, she thought to herself. *I'll speak to the people who live there and ask them for directions back to my village!*

'Hello! Is there anybody there?' Sylvan called out as she made her way towards the house. There was no answer.

As Sylvan drew nearer, she saw that the kitchen (which was at the side of the house) was empty and that the door of the house was closed. However, she saw that there was an open window and she was able to see inside.

'Hello!' she called again. 'Is anyone home?' No one answered.

Sylvan hoisted herself up through the window and into the house. On the table there was some cassava bread. Hungry now, Sylvan broke a piece off and ate it. Then, tired after all the walking, she fell asleep.

Meanwhile, Sylvan's husband, Amos, and the other villagers had begun to worry about Sylvan. It had been hours since they had left her. Wondering where she could have got to, they made their way back to the lakeside where Sylvan had stopped for a rest, but when they arrived of course Sylvan was nowhere to be found. They searched everywhere for her.

'Sylvan! Sylvan!' they called. But she was too far away to hear them.

The villagers knew that anyone who was separated from a travelling group would make their own way back home. Amos and the villagers began to think that was what Sylvan must have done. 'Perhaps when she couldn't find us she went back home!' Amos said to the others. Everyone agreed that that was what Sylvan had done, so they decided to continue on their journey, believing that Sylvan was safe at home.

Some time passed and Sylvan woke from her sleep. As she did so she heard the sound of someone approaching the house.

'What a life . . . what a life . . .' she heard the person mumble. Whoever it was stopped outside the kitchen and when Sylvan peeped out of the window she could see a strange little man carrying a string of fish.

She called out to him, 'Hello, I'm lost. Could you tell me the way to get home?'

Karahu was startled, but on seeing her he remembered straight away the wish that the colourful stone had granted him and he knew at once that this woman was the wife he had wished for.

'Home?' he said. 'But my dear, you are home! You are the wife I have been waiting for!'

Was this man mad? Sylvan couldn't believe what she was hearing!

'Wife?' she scoffed. 'I already have a husband and I already have a home and I am not staying here!' Sylvan ran out of the house as fast as she could. Karahu watched as she disappeared into the darkness and chuckled. He wasn't worried at all that she wouldn't come back, as he was sure his wish had come true. Sylvan ran and ran but it was no good, she didn't know where she was going and all she could see around her was darkness. She would have to go back to the little man's house until she could work out how to get home.

When she returned, Karahu felt very pleased with himself. He had finished cleaning his fish and prepared supper for two. He set the table and he waited for Sylvan to join him. Sylvan could smell the wonderful aromas of the tasty fish supper that Karahu had made and she felt very hungry. But she did not want to share a supper with this strange little man who wanted to claim her for his wife, so she refused to eat.

'No worries,' Karahu said smugly. 'When your belly gripes, you will eat!'

'Never!' said Sylvan. 'I will never eat your food!'

The next day, when Karahu went fishing, Sylvan tried to

see if she could find a way to get home, but every time she wandered out of the house she ended up back where she started. When Karahu returned, Sylvan refused to eat once more and the day after that she did the same again. On the third day, however, Sylvan could bear it no longer. She was very weak. Her belly was rumbling loudly and she was very, very hungry. She needed to build up her strength so she could keep searching for a way out, so she joined Karahu at his table and she ate the fish supper.

After that, each evening they ate together in silence and this went on for weeks and months. But Karahu wanted more than just sitting at a table in silence with an unhappy woman. He wanted a family.

So one evening Karahu cooked a special fish broth for Sylvan and as he cooked it he blew kisses into the pot and chanted some words over the food:

> *'As you eat my delicious broth,*
> *We are forever bound together.*
> *Before this year has come and gone*
> *You will bear for me a son.'*

'Now you will stay here with me forever!' said Karahu gleefully and Sylvan wept. She hoped above all hopes that one day her husband, Amos, would find her, for she still loved him very much. But, alas, as time went by the spell that Karahu had cast over the food finally began to work and before long Sylvan came to bear Karahu a son.

Back in the village Sylvan's husband, Amos, had not given up on her, though a whole year had passed. There was not a day that went by without Amos trying to find his missing wife. Everybody in the village knew about Sylvan's disappearance but nobody knew how to help. That is until one day a wise old woman, who knew just about everything about anything, came to find Amos and told him all that had happened.

'Your wife is living with a grumpy little man who goes by the name of Karahu,' said the wise old woman. 'They live together in a house above the lake. She has even borne him a child. If you want to get her back, this is what you must do. Go to the house in the daytime and there you will find her alone, because Karahu spends all day fishing. She will follow you, but before you take her away you must know how to break the spell that Karahu has cast on her. If not, then Karahu will only follow you and take her back. Be sure to find the colourful stone that your wife threw down between the lake and the house. When you find it, break a little piece off and carry it with you. When you find your wife and you're about to leave Karahu's house, ask your wife to blow a kiss in the living room, blow a kiss in the bedroom, blow kisses all around the house and blow a kiss outside in the kitchen. Then place the colourful stone where the child sleeps, take your wife and go!'

Well, Amos set out straight away. He walked on and on, until at last he reached the lake. He found the colourful stone that his wife had dropped between the lake and the house and he knocked it against a rock until a piece broke away. Then, carrying the piece of the colourful stone with him as he had been told to do, he followed where the stone led him, singing:

> 'Clap hands and slap my thighs,
> Clap hands and slap my thighs,
> Clap hands and slap my thighs,
> I'll be on my way . . .'

Eventually he could see a small house in the distance.

Sylvan, alone in the house, could hear the singing and she recognized Amos's voice immediately. She ran to meet him. They were so pleased to see each other!

'Quickly,' she said, 'let's get away from this place before Karahu returns and finds you here.' But Amos, remembering what the wise old woman had told him, carried on walking towards the house. 'First we have to break the spell that Karahu has cast over you,' he insisted. He asked his wife to blow a kiss in the living room, blow a kiss in the bedroom, blow kisses all around the house and blow a kiss outside in the kitchen, just as the wise old woman had told him. Then Amos put the piece of the colourful stone beside the sleeping child and took his wife and went away.

Shortly afterwards Karahu returned carrying a string of fish as usual. He went straight to the kitchen and called Sylvan. 'Yes, Karahu!' Sylvan's voice replied from the living room inside the house, but when Karahu followed the voice to where it was coming from, Sylvan was not there. Karahu called Sylvan again. 'Yes, Karahu!' Sylvan's voice called back. This time Sylvan's voice was coming from the bedroom. Karahu followed the sound of her voice to the bedroom, but when he got there Sylvan was not there. Karahu called and called and went from one room to the next, but Sylvan was not to be found anywhere. Finally he called again, 'Sylvan! Wife, where are you?' And from outside in the kitchen Sylvan's voice answered, 'Here I am, Karahu! Come!' So he went out to the kitchen to find her, but Sylvan was not there. Karahu finally realized that he had been tricked. He was furious. He stamped his feet and made so much noise he woke up the baby.

'Aha,' Karahu said. 'At least I still have my son!' Karahu followed the sound of the baby's voice to the child's bed, but as he drew near to the child Karahu could see once again he had been tricked. Glowing on the child's pillow was the piece of the colourful stone, and there where the baby should have been was a colourful bird.

'What a life . . . what a life . . .' Karahu sobbed and the bird flew up to him making the prettiest chirping sound Karahu had ever heard. 'I am Kingfisher!' sang the bird. 'Let me stay with you . . .' And from that day on, Karahu had the company he had longed for and he never went fishing alone again.

Too Choosy-Choosy

This story is based on a folk tale from Guyana

There was once a king who had a daughter named Verona. Princess Verona was very beautiful. She would spend her days in front of the mirror admiring her beauty. Verona was a spoilt princess who always got everything she wanted, and everything she wanted had to be the best. If it wasn't the best then she would moan and groan. That was how it had always been. Her father, the king, would try and get the best of anything she asked for but she was never satisfied.

'You too choosy-choosy!' her father, the king, would say. 'One day you'll choose and choose and you'll lose.' But Verona didn't care what her father said. She just pleased herself and continued being choosy.

When it was time for Verona to find a husband she decided that she would only accept the perfect husband and nothing less. Tired of his daughter's constant moaning, the king took it upon himself to find the perfect husband for his daughter.

'I am looking for a husband for my daughter, Verona,' the king told his people, 'and only the perfect suitor will do.'

News travelled far and wide. Soon everyone knew that the king was looking for the perfect husband for his daughter and before long a line of well-to-do suitors presented themselves to the king and the princess but the princess was not interested in any of them.

The first was too tall, the second too short, another too fat, another too thin. The princess wanted a man who was just the perfect size and with the perfect face, and when she found one who was the perfect size with the perfect face he was too boring or he talked too much or he spoke too little or he didn't give her enough attention. Whatever excuse Verona could find, she did. The bottom line was that none of the suitors were perfect enough to be her husband and the king didn't know what to do.

'There must be somebody out there that's perfect for you!' he said, and Verona just smiled.

'If I don't find the perfect man, then I will just have to live with you forever,' she said happily. This worried the king. This worried the king a lot. He could think of nothing worse than spending the rest of his days trying to please his daughter and he hoped beyond hope that one day someone perfect would come along and take her off his hands.

Living in the village was a humble fisherman named Sam. Every morning Sam would deliver a load of fish to the palace and, every morning from her balcony, Verona would watch this fine figure of a man carry the boxes of fish across the courtyard to the palace kitchens, and she would admire his perfect dark brown skin and his perfect smile with perfect white teeth and she would listen to his perfect laugh and she would say, 'Good morning, Sam.'

When he answered 'Good morning, Princess Verona!' in his perfect deep voice, her heart would race. But before she could catch her breath and speak further he would be on his way. Although she liked the look of him, she knew that Sam was much too poor to be the perfect husband for a princess. Nevertheless, Princess Verona was curious about the fisherman and she wanted to know more about him. He looked like such a nice fellow.

One morning Princess Verona was determined to speak to Sam so, instead of watching him from her balcony, she waited for Sam in the courtyard. As he came to deliver the fish as usual she jumped out and startled him.

'Good morning, Sam,' she said.

Sam almost dropped his fish. 'Oh . . . Good morning, Princess Verona,' he said politely. 'I'm sorry, I wasn't expecting to see you there!'

'I know,' said Princess Verona. 'I came down here especially as you are always in so much of a hurry and I never get to speak to you.'

Sam was taken aback by her interest in him.

'Oh, I'm sorry,' he said. 'I have so much fish to deliver in the mornings. Please accept my apologies.'

Princess Verona blushed. No one had ever made her blush before but there was something about this fisherman that made her giddy. That morning Princess Verona and Sam the fisherman spoke and laughed about all sorts of things and, the more Princess Verona spoke to him, the more she liked him. The more he spoke to her, the more he liked her too. From that day on, every morning Princess Verona waited in the courtyard for Sam to arrive with the fish and every morning they chatted about this and that and enjoyed each other's company.

The king was very glad to see his daughter having so much fun with the young fisherman and one day he called his daughter aside and said, 'Verona, could this be him? Is Sam the fisherman the perfect man for you? Would he be the perfect husband?'

Verona ummed and ahhed. 'Well . . . umm . . . ahh . . . umm . . .' and finally she said, 'No. How can I marry a poor fisherman? I'm a princess! He's not perfect enough for me.'

'You too choosy-choosy!' said the king. 'One day you'll choose and choose and you'll lose.' The king was angry. He wondered if he would ever get rid of his fussy daughter.

Then one day, quite out of the blue, a handsome gentleman riding a strong black stallion arrived at the palace gates. The gentleman looked amazing, dressed in a crisp white suit and a fine cane hat. His height looked perfect. His face looked perfect. He was rich and charming too.

'Good day!' he said. 'My name is Camo.'

The princess immediately took a liking to him. He said all the right things and seemed to know exactly how to act to show the princess that he would make a perfect husband for her. He spoke of his wealth and his magnificent castle and he told her how he could lavish her with the most expensive jewellery. Princess Verona fell in love with him immediately.

He came to visit every day and when he asked the king for Verona's hand in marriage, the king turned to his daughter and said, 'Verona, could this be him? Is this fine gentleman, Camo, the perfect man for you? Would he be the perfect husband?'

Verona ummed and ahhed.

'Well . . . umm . . . ahh . . . umm . . .' Finally she said: 'Yes! This is the perfect man for me.'

The king was overjoyed. He began to make plans for the wedding straight away and he asked the gentleman suitor to come back the following week to marry his daughter.

When Sam the fisherman heard about the engagement of Princess Verona to a fine gentleman called Camo, he was very sad. He had known all along that, being a poor fisherman, he didn't stand a chance of marrying Princess Verona, but deep down in his heart he had hoped that by some miracle his dream would come true. But, alas, it wasn't to be.

Sam was so distraught that he stayed in bed for three whole days and he was unable to get up and work. Sam was still in bed when one of the servants to the king arrived at his small fisherman's hut asking for a special order of fish for the wedding banquet. Sam was about to turn the servant away when he had a thought. Maybe if he showed up at the palace with the order of fish and Princess Verona was to see him again she would come to her senses and call the wedding off! So he agreed to deliver the fish on the morning of the wedding, in the hope that seeing him might change Verona's mind.

The wedding morning arrived and Sam entered the palace through the courtyard. Up on the balcony Princess Verona saw him arrive. Her heart skipped a beat but she pretended that it did not bother her to see him – she was going to be married to the perfect man that afternoon after all.

'Good morning,' said Sam. Princess Verona did not answer. She could not. Seeing Sam had confused her. She just waved and went inside. Deep down in her heart she was afraid she might be still in love with him . . . but how could she be when she was about to marry the perfect man?

Sam carried the boxes of fish to the palace kitchen. There was so much fish he had to cross the courtyard several times. Each time he crossed the courtyard Sam looked up on the balcony to see if Princess Verona was there but she was nowhere to be seen. After the last box had been delivered Sam left, convinced now that any dream of marrying Princess Verona was well and truly dashed. As he walked away Verona peeped from behind a pillar on the balcony and watched him go. But it was too late. Camo, her husband-to-be, would be arriving very soon to marry her.

Sam could see a glittering horse-drawn carriage coming towards the palace. Inside it was the man Sam thought must be Verona's fiancé, Camo. Sam decided to wait around to have a good look at the man Verona intended to marry. The man got out of the carriage and Sam bid him good day, wishing him well on his wedding day. None the wiser, Camo thanked him and entered the palace.

Sam took a disliking to him straight away. Perhaps this was natural, since the man was about to marry the only girl he had ever truly loved. But looking into Camo's piercing green eyes had sent a shiver down Sam's spine.

He decided he would hang around a little bit longer. He wanted to make sure that Verona really was going to marry the perfect man.

Hiding behind a palace wall, Sam secretly watched all the guests arrive for the wedding. When the final guest had arrived and the wedding was about to begin, Sam slipped into the palace and mingled with the guests unnoticed. All the time his eyes were firmly fixed on Verona. It almost broke his heart to see the beautiful Verona exchange wedding vows with the strange man. Sam had hoped and dreamed that he would have been the one exchanging wedding vows with Verona on their special day and it hurt him deeply. When the ring was placed on Verona's finger, it hurt him so much he thought he would never breathe again.

When the service was over and the merriment began, Sam thought he would take a closer look at Verona's new husband. He watched as others congratulated him with a handshake and he waited in line for his turn, and when he got up close he was disturbed by the green hue on the man's skin. What was it? It reminded Sam of the colour of the deepest ocean. Why had nobody else noticed how odd the colour of his skin was? And when Sam shook his hand he was not ready for the rough leathery texture of it and it scared him. Unable to keep his concerns to himself any longer, Sam approached the king quietly.

'Your Highness, please may I have a word?'

'Sam . . . I wasn't expecting to see you here! Is everything all right?'

'No. You must get your daughter away from that man. He is not right for her!' Sam said.

Of course, the king thought that Sam's jealousy was getting the better of him. He tried to calm Sam down.

'Now don't make a fool of yourself, young man! My daughter is happily married now, so off you go, be on your way . . .' and he had his servants throw Sam out of the palace.

Sam didn't know what to do next. Suddenly he spotted the glittering carriage waiting outside ready to take Verona and her new husband to their new home. He decided to attach himself to the back of the carriage and hide there so he could go with them when they left.

The time came for Verona and her new husband to leave. The king and all the guests waved them off and wished them well, and the glittering carriage set off. From inside Princess Verona blew a final kiss to her father and he wiped a tear from his eye. As much as he wanted to be rid of her because of her fussiness, he knew he would miss her, as he loved her very much. As they left, Verona's eyes seemed to search the crowd for someone else. But she couldn't see Sam anywhere.

It was a long and uncomfortable ride to Camo's home. Sam held on to the back of the glittering carriage for dear life and, inside, Verona grew tired and slept for part of the way. When she woke up, she expected to be at her new husband's magnificent castle but instead the carriage pulled up at a miserable-looking shack surrounded by bushes and tangled vines. She thought they must have taken a wrong turning and become lost.

'Home sweet home!' said Camo, her husband.

'Home?' said Verona. 'What do you mean? Where's your castle?'

'I don't have one!' laughed Camo. 'I lied!' At once he grabbed her with his rough scaly green hands and began to drag her out of the carriage. 'I'm Camoudi Snake and I heard you were looking for the perfect husband, so I disguised myself and I fooled you into believing I was him!'

'Ouch! You're hurting me! Let me go!' screamed Verona. But the horrible snake would not let her go.

'You heard what she said!' said Sam, jumping down from the back of the carriage. 'Let her go!'

Camoudi was taken entirely by surprise. Verona, too, was shocked but very pleased to see him. Sam immediately tried to break Verona free from the grip of Camoudi's hand but the cunning snake held on tightly and would not let go.

Camoudi opened up his big snake mouth and was about to gobble up Princess Verona when Sam got out his sharp fisherman's knife and in one swift movement sliced off Camoudi's head, setting Verona free.

'Oh, Sam, I'm so sorry!' cried Verona. 'I was too choosy-choosy. If only I hadn't been so foolish and I had followed my heart, none of this would have happened!'

But Sam was so happy to have Verona back and away from the wicked grip of Camoudi that he forgave her and asked her to marry him, and Princess Verona didn't umm or ahh, she said 'Yes' straight away.

Two Dinners

*Based on an Ashanti story brought
over to the Caribbean*

People say there was a time long ago when animals were different from how they are now. Many animals walked on two feet, as humans do, and they spoke with words.

Brer Anansi, the mischievous spider, was one such creature and though he had eight legs he too spoke with words.

Brer Anansi liked to go to parties. He liked to make sure, if there was something going on – a party or a feast or some celebration or other – that he would be in the midst of it, enjoying himself. Most of all, Brer Anansi liked to dance. He believed he was the best dancer out of all the animals, and loved to show off what he could do. This made him very popular, so he was always being invited to parties.

Now Brer Dog and Brer Goat each decided to have a party. It just so happened that both parties were to happen on the same day.

'My wife is going to be cooking up a fine feast!' said Brer Dog.

'Oh, what is she cooking?' asked Brer Anansi.

'Fried chicken with rice and peas and plantain, with coconut cake and custard for afters,' said Brer Dog.

Brer Anansi liked to eat. Some folks called him greedy but all Brer Anansi would say to them was that he simply liked to eat good food, and lots of it.

'That sure sounds like a good dinner. I'll come to your party!' Brer Anansi told Brer Dog.

'Good. My party is tomorrow and it starts at three o'clock. I live in the West Village,' Brer Dog said, handing Brer Anansi a note with his address on it.

'No problem,' said Brer Anansi.

Not long later, Brer Goat approached Brer Anansi and invited him to *his* party.

Brer Anansi answered the same way. 'What is your wife cooking?'

'Callaloo, lobster and pepper soup with dumplings, and she's even making some chocolate ice cream.'

'That sure sounds like a good dinner. I'll come to your party!' Brer Anansi told Brer Goat.

'Good. My party is tomorrow and it starts at three o'clock. I live in the East Village,' Brer Goat said.

'No problem,' said Brer Anansi, although he knew there most definitely was one.

Never before had Anansi been invited to two parties on the same day, at the same time. This was going to be difficult, especially considering the parties were at opposite ends of the island. Folks began to wonder how Brer Anansi was going to decide which party to go to.

The next morning, Brer Anansi rose bright and early and put on his good suit. It so happened that some of Brer Anansi's children had fallen sick so Brer Anansi's wife had told him that she would not be joining him that day.

'Can I come? Can I come?' cried Kuma and Kwek, the two children that were well. They got dressed quickly and accompanied their father.

'Don't bother to cook any supper for us,' Brer Anansi told his wife. 'I am sure we'll be full from eating two dinners when we come home this evening!'

So Brer Anansi set off to go to the parties with his two sons, Kuma and Kwek.

Most animals in the village had been invited to one of the parties, so they all came out of their houses around the same time and walked along the main road with Brer Anansi and his boys.

'It sure is going to be a good party at Brer Dog's home!' said Brer Turtle.

'Brer Goat's party is going to be better,' Brer Cockerel said. Brer Anansi laughed and bragged about how he had been invited to both and how he was going to have a better time than all of them.

For most of the journey, the route to both parties was the same way and all of the animals chatted together and shared their excitement as they walked. Eventually they reached the crossroads where a big sign said WEST VILLAGE TO THE LEFT. EAST VILLAGE TO THE RIGHT. It was here that those who were going to Brer Dog's party went to the left, down the West Road to the West Village, and those who were going to Brer Goat's party went to the right, down the East Road to the East Village. Finally, it was only Brer Anansi and his two sons that remained, trying to work out which way to go first.

'I'll go to Brer Dog's party first,' said Brer Anansi, finally making a decision. He told his boys to follow him down the West Road to the West Village.

'I sure am looking forward to that fried chicken,' Brer Anansi said.

'Me too!' said Kuma and Kwek.

And the three of them walked a little way down the West Road. Then suddenly Brer Anansi stopped.

'I've had a thought,' he said. 'Maybe we should go to

Brer Goat's party first. That callaloo, lobster and pepper soup with dumplings will surely start off the rest of the food just right.' Kuma and Kwek agreed. 'Turn around, boys! Let's go to Brer Goat's house first.'

So Brer Anansi and his boys turned back and walked until they got back to the crossroads, and when they reached it they took the East Road leading to the East Village.

A little way down the East Road, Brer Anansi stopped again.

'Brer Dog's wife's coconut cake sure is calling me!' he said and he told the boys to turn around again so that they could get back to the crossroads and take the West Road to Dog's house in the West Village. This happened several times with Brer Anansi changing his mind about which party to go to first. One minute it was Brer Dog's and the next it was Brer Goat's. The boys weren't happy with Brer Anansi changing his mind all the time. Their legs were getting tired and they were feeling frustrated.

'We must go to the party that is serving food first,' said Brer Anansi, coming up with another idea, 'and after we have eaten there, then we will go to the second party.'

'How will we know which party is serving food first?' asked Kuma.

'Supposing we choose to go to one first and when we get there we find they've already eaten?' said Kwek.

Brer Anansi thought Kwek had made a good point.

That would be disastrous. Brer Anansi certainly didn't want to miss out on any of the dinners.

'I'll think of something . . .' said Brer Anansi but he was running out of ideas. By this time the children were tired and hungry.

Then Kuma had an idea.

'Father, you can send Kwek and me to the parties ahead of you! I will go to the fried chicken party in the West Village' – Kuma loved fried chicken – 'and Kwek can go to the chocolate ice cream party in the East Village.'

'No' said Kwek, 'I'll go to the fried chicken party and you go to the chocolate ice cream one!'

'No,' said Kuma, 'it's my idea so I'll go . . .'

'Hush!' said Brer Anansi. 'I think it's a good idea for you two to go on ahead. When you get to the parties, let me know when they are serving dinner and the party that is serving dinner first is the one I will go to!'

It was finally agreed between them that Kuma would go to Brer Dog's party in the West Village and Kwek would go to Brer Goat's party in the East Village. All Brer Anansi had to do now was to come up with a plan for the boys to signal their father and let him know which party's dinner was being served first.

'Go home and get me two long ropes,' Brer Anansi said to his sons. The boys did as they were told and when they returned Brer Anansi stood in the centre of the crossroads, halfway between the two villages, and tied the end of both ropes around his waist. He gave the other end of the first rope to Kuma and the other end of the second rope to Kwek.

Then he said to Kuma, 'Follow the West Road to the West Village and go to Brer Dog's party.'

And to Kwek he said, 'Follow the East Road to the East Village and go to Brer Goat's party.'

And to both of them he said, 'When food is being served, I want you to pull on the rope, hard.' That way Brer Anansi would know which party was serving food first and he would be pulled in the direction of that party immediately.

So Kuma went to the West Village and Kwek went to the East Village as Brer Anansi had instructed them to do, and Brer Anansi waited at the crossroads for the signal.

When Kuma reached Brer Dog's party in the West Village the music was playing loudly and people were dancing and having a good time. Before long Kuma was joining in with them. He was a great dancer as he had learnt a few steps from his father. After the dancing, the guests at the party played games, sang songs and joked around. Kuma enjoyed taking part in all the festivities. It was a great party, but Kuma never once let go of the rope that his father had asked him to hold.

Kwek was also having a good time at Brer Goat's party in the East Village. There too the music was playing loud and people were dancing and having a good time. Kwek was the life and soul of the party and taking the centre of attention, as his father would have done, with his fancy footwork on the dance floor. The guests at Brer Goat's party played games, sang songs and joked around, just like the ones at Brer Dog's party were doing, and Kwek enjoyed taking part in all the festivities, just like his brother at Brer Dog's party. Kwek obediently kept hold of the rope just like his father had asked him to do.

Meanwhile, at the crossroads, Brer Anansi was getting bored and hungry. He was dressed in his good suit ready to go to a party with nothing to do but wait for the signal. He waited and waited, getting hungrier and hungrier, and more and more bored.

At about four thirty Brer Goat stopped the party in the East Village and announced that dinner was about to be served. At about the same time over at Brer Dog's party in the West Village, Brer Dog's wife announced that the fried chicken was ready and people could eat. Kuma and Kwek, remembering what their father had told them to do, started to pull on the rope straight away, Kuma from the West Village and Kwek from the East Village. As they pulled on the rope Brer Anansi, still standing at the crossroads, felt the tug from them on either side. As each son pulled on the rope from east and west Brer Anansi could not move in one direction or the other. He was stuck. He tried to move to the west side but he could not budge and he tried to move to the east side but he could not do it. Kuma and Kwek pulled harder and harder to try to get their father to the party in time for the food, but the more they pulled, the more he could not move from the crossroads.

As he pulled on the rope Kuma decided he might as well fill his belly with some of Ma Dog's fried chicken with rice and peas and plantain, followed by coconut cake and custard for afters. He enjoyed every bit. The party music continued and, still pulling on the rope, Kuma danced the night away. Kwek too filled his belly with Brer Goat's delicious callaloo, lobster and pepper soup with dumplings and finished with some chocolate ice cream. He kept pulling on the rope the whole time as he danced into the night. Kuma and Kwek only stopped pulling on the rope when the party was over. Kuma thanked Brer Dog and his wife and started back home. Kwek thanked Brer Goat for giving him such a wonderful time and he started back on his journey home too. When Kuma and Kwek got to the crossroads where their father was waiting they found him in the same spot where they had left him. But because they had pulled on the ropes so hard, it had made Brer Anansi's waist extra thin, and his body had puffed out like two balloons above and below the waist. (And from that day on, that's how Brer Anansi looked – and how he still looks today.) The children did their best not to laugh and tried their hardest not to show how good a time they had both had at the parties they had been to.

'The more you both pulled on the rope, the more I couldn't move!' said Brer Anansi angrily. 'And now I'm hurting all over, and I'm *hungry*!'

The boys took Brer Anansi home and when he got there he was so vexed he started to yell at his wife, 'Where's my dinner?'

But there wasn't any food for him because he'd told his wife not to cook. So Brer Anansi went to bed on an empty belly that night, all because he was too greedy and he couldn't make up his mind about which party to go to.

The Three Tasks

This story is based on a French Caribbean folk tale

There was once a beautiful young girl called Avaline who was left in the care of her stepfather after the death of her mother. On her sickbed, Avaline's mother gave Avaline a gift. It was a small, funny, knobbly-looking twig.

'Soon I will leave you,' said Avaline's mother. 'Here is your protection when I am gone. This is a magical twig and when it is used by the person who truly loves you it will save you from harm. Remember: nothing can stand in the way of true love.' Avaline was too upset to understand what her mother was telling her and she simply wept as she hugged her.

The stepfather didn't like Avaline very much and, soon after Avaline's mother died, he started being cruel to her. He made her his servant. Anything he told her to do, she had to do it. He was so wicked that he would beat her if she refused. Avaline dreamed of being far away from her evil stepfather and living a happy life.

One day Avaline was busy washing clothes in the river when she was joined by a handsome young man called François. Avaline and François spoke all afternoon and it felt as if they had known one another forever. They laughed and chatted and felt so comfortable in each other's company.

From then on, each day François would return to the river and join Avaline as she did her washing. Avaline and François gradually fell in love.

François was so overcome with his love for Avaline that he asked her to marry him. She was overjoyed and was happy to accept his proposal but, in order to marry Avaline, Francois would have to ask her stepfather for permission, as that was the custom in those days. Avaline suspected her stepfather would not approve as he was a cruel man and wanted her to be his slave forever. Nevertheless, one day, after she had finished her washing, Avaline led François to her home.

Once there, François respectfully asked Avaline's stepfather if he could have her hand in marriage. The mean stepfather wasn't happy. In fact, he was furious! If

Avaline were to marry this man, who would he get to do all his chores? The cooking, the cleaning, the washing? Avaline thought the evil stepfather would surely say no and she would be enslaved by him forever. But to her surprise, the cunning stepfather turned to the handsome young man and said, 'I am a reasonable man. Of course you have my permission to marry her. But first you must complete three tasks. Once you have completed all three tasks successfully then you can marry my stepdaughter.'

Avaline immediately suspected that her stepfather was up to something and doubted that the tasks he set would be straightforward. Still, she was glad the young man had been given a chance, as slim as it might be.

'I must speak to you privately,' said the stepfather to François and he sent Avaline off to do some housework.

Once he and François were alone, the stepfather turned to him and said, 'If you do not complete the tasks successfully, you must go away and never return to bother my stepdaughter again.' The young suitor reluctantly agreed that if he failed to complete the tasks successfully then he would go away and never return.

Then the wicked stepfather went to the kitchen and took a bucket from under the sink. With a sharp knife, he pierced the bucket several times until it was full of holes.

'For the first task, I want you to take this bucket to the river,' said the evil stepfather. 'I want you to fill it with water from the river, bring the bucket of water to my house and fill my water tank with the water you have carried.'

The river was quite a way away from the stepfather's house and François knew that there was no way he could collect water from the river with a bucket full of holes and still have water in it when he returned.

'But that will be impossible!' said François. 'The water will leak out of the holes in the bucket before I reach your house.'

'So it will,' said the stepfather smugly, 'but that's your problem.'

François felt frustrated. It seemed that he would never get to marry the girl he had fallen in love with after all. Still, he took the bucket full of holes and he made his way to the river. Once he was there he put the bucket in the river to fill it and, as he took it out again, just as he had expected, water was already leaking from the many holes. As quickly as he could, François ran all the way back to the house to fill the water tank with the little water he had left in the bucket. Alas, when François reached the house, the bucket had lost all the water and was empty.

But François would not give up. His love for Avaline was so strong, and he wanted to marry her more than anything in the world, so he went back to the river. This time, after he had dipped the bucket full of holes in the river, he ran even faster back to the house. But still there wasn't a drop of water left in the bucket when he arrived at the water tank.

Avaline came back from doing her chores and she watched François making his trips to the river and back again, running faster and faster each time with the bucket full of holes.

'What are you doing?' she asked.

'Your stepfather has asked me to fill this bucket with water from the river and then to bring the bucket of water to his water tank and fill the tank with the water I collect.'

'But the bucket is full of holes!' said Avaline. 'It's impossible!'

'I know,' said François, 'but I want to marry you! So I'll keep trying.'

'You must truly love me,' Avaline said and, remembering the special gift that her mother had given her, she took it out of her purse.

'My mother left me this but I am unable to use it. The magic will only work when used by someone who truly loves me . . .'

'And what must I do with it?' asked François.

But before Avaline could answer, the magic twig spoke. 'Strike me on the ground three times!'

François was confused but he loved Avaline so much so he did as the twig said.

'Now you must tap the water tank three times,' the

magic twig said. The young man ran to the water tank and tapped it three times.

'Now go to the river and dip me in the river.' François went to the river and put the tip of the wand in the river.

Then the twig said, 'Repeat after me, *River, fill the tank!*'

François repeated the words: 'River, fill the tank!'

'Your task is done!' said the twig.

'Really?' François said.

'Yes,' said the twig. 'Go and see for yourself.'

François went back to the stepfather's house, and lo and behold the water tank was full of river water! The young man called the stepfather and told him that he had completed the task. He showed him the full water tank.

The stepfather was shocked. 'Fine,' he said angrily, 'but you still have two more tasks to do! For your second task I want you to . . .' (the stepfather thought long and hard) '. . . dry up the river so I can walk across it.'

François sighed. He knew this time he had no chance of completing the task.

'But that will be impossible!' said François. 'How am I to dry up the river?'

'That's *your* problem,' said the wicked stepfather.

François went sadly to the river. As he sat down, feeling sorry for himself, Avaline came and sat beside him.

'What has he asked you to do this time?' she asked.

'Your stepfather has set me an even more impossible task. He has asked me to dry up the river so he can walk across it,' François said. 'Do you think the magic twig can help again?'

Avaline smiled. She was sure it could. She took out her mother's magic twig again. As before, the twig spoke and told François to strike it in the river three times. François took the twig and did as he was told.

'Now repeat after me, *River, empty yourself!*'

François repeated the words: 'River, empty yourself!'

And as he did so the river water began to lower.

'The river water is going down!' François exclaimed. The river water got lower and lower until the river was dry.

'Your task is done!' said the twig. 'Go and get Avaline's stepfather.'

So François went to the house and asked the stepfather to follow him down to the river.

The stepfather laughed. 'You don't expect me to believe that you have actually emptied the river, do you?' he said. But when he arrived at the river and saw that all the water had gone he stopped laughing immediately. He had no idea how François had done it.

'No! This cannot be!' he shouted.

'Walk across it,' said François. 'The river is dry, just as you requested.'

The evil stepfather climbed into the dry river and he walked across it. He was furious.

'So you have managed to fill my water tank with river

water carried in a bucket full of holes, and you have managed to dry up the river so I can walk across it. But you will never be able to do this final task! Never!'

François was worried. He knew that this time the evil stepfather would set a task so difficult that even the magic twig would struggle to achieve it.

'What is the final task that you would like me to do?' he asked.

'Let me think . . .' said the stepfather. He thought and thought and thought. 'In fact, let me sleep on it,' he said. 'Come back to my house tomorrow and I will tell you your task then.'

François agreed that he would come back the next day and he left.

All night the evil stepfather tossed and turned as he tried to think of the most impossible task to set for François.

When he awoke the next morning he had in his mind the perfect, most impossible task. It wasn't long before François arrived.

'For your third task,' said the stepfather, 'you must go to the ice tree by the ice lake and get the two golden eggs that are at the top of the tree. Bring them to me by noon today!'

Now the ice tree was a special tree known to be impossible to climb because of its slippery and icy surface. At the top of the tree were two precious golden eggs.

François sighed. He knew he had no chance of getting the golden eggs.

'But that will be impossible!' said François. 'How am I to climb the icy, slippery tree to get to the golden eggs?'

'That's *your* problem,' said the wicked stepfather.

Disheartened, François made his way to the ice lake on the edge of which the ice tree stood. He tried to climb the tree, but try as he might the surface of the tree's trunk was too slippery and he kept sliding back down. François was sitting at the bottom of the tree feeling sorry for himself when Avaline came and sat beside him.

'There you are. I've been looking all over for you,' she said.

'Your stepfather has given me a truly impossible task,' François said. 'At the top of the ice tree are two golden eggs. He wants me to bring them to him by noon, but every time I try to climb the ice tree I slide back down again. Not even the magic twig can help me this time.'

'Of course I can!' said the twig. 'I can help you. You must breathe on Avaline three times and say a spell and she will die.'

'Die?' François gasped. 'But I don't want Avaline to die!'

'She will only stay dead for a short time,' said the magic twig. 'After you breathe on her three times, you must say this spell:

Bones, be my ladder to climb the tree!

'Then when she is dead on the ground, you must take her bones out of her body and use them to make a ladder. Lean the ladder against the tree and use it to climb up to the two golden eggs at the top. You must then take the two golden eggs and climb back down the ladder. Once you reach the bottom of the tree, breathe on her three times again and say,

Bones, return!

and her bones will go back into her body and she will be alive again.'

François wasn't sure if this was a good idea. He was afraid that if he made a mistake and got the spell wrong he might not be able to bring Avaline back to life.

'I think it's too risky,' said François. 'I don't want to lose Avaline.'

'And I don't want to lose you either,' said Avaline, 'which is why you must do this for me.'

Eventually Avaline managed to convince François that it was the only way they would have a chance to be together. François agreed that he would do it.

François concentrated hard on all the instructions the twig had given him.

First he had to breathe on her three times and say the spell:

'Bones, be my ladder to climb the tree!'

Then he had to take Avaline's bones out of her body and use them to make a ladder. He had to climb the ladder and get the two golden eggs at the top of the tree then climb down again, breathe on her three times and say,

'Bones return!'

After that, her bones would return to her body and she would be alive again. So once he was sure what he had to do, François did everything the twig had told him and he got the two golden eggs from the top of the ice tree. Then he climbed down again, breathed on Avaline three times and said,

'Bones, return!'

And, just as the twig had told him, Avaline's bones returned to her body and she was alive again.

It was eleven thirty and François knew he had to bring the eggs to the stepfather by midday. He didn't have much time left. Just as they were about to leave and bring the golden eggs to the wicked stepfather, Avaline noticed that one of the bones in her little finger was missing.

'Oh no, I must have left it at the top of the tree!' François said.

'You must go and get it,' said Avaline. 'Hurry!' So François, remembering the spell, breathed on her three times again and said,

'Bones, be my ladder to climb the tree!'

And Avaline fell down dead.

Then he took the bones from her body to make a ladder. He climbed the ladder and found the bone from her little finger at the top of the tree. Quickly he climbed down the ladder again. Once François reached the bottom of the tree, he breathed on Avaline three times and said,

'Bones, return!'

Avaline's bones went back into her body and she was alive again. It was mere minutes before noon so they ran back to the house.

'My three tasks are done!' François said, giving the two golden eggs to the evil stepfather. The stepfather was shocked to see that François had completed the third and final task. He had no idea how he had completed all three, and he was furious.

'You have managed to fill my water tank with river water carried in a bucket full of holes,' said the stepfather. 'You have managed to dry up the river so I can walk across it, and you have also brought me the two golden eggs from the top of the ice tree. I have no more tasks for you. As I promised, you may take my stepdaughter as your wife.' And though the stepfather wasn't happy for them to do so, he reluctantly kept his word. Avaline and François got married and lived happily ever after.

The Race Between Toad and Donkey

This story is based on a folk tale from Jamaica

There was always one kind of competition or other going on between the animals on the savannah. This day was no different. This day Donkey and Toad were arguing about which one of them could beat the other in a race.

'Eee-aww, ee-aww,' laughed Donkey. 'Your legs are so small compared to mine. There is no way you can beat me in a race!'

Toad refused to be thrown by the mocking jeers of Donkey. He was not going to be openly ridiculed in front of the whole village. All the animals had already started to gather round, itching to see what all the commotion was about.

'Don't stand for it, Toad!' Fowl called. 'Show him you're a bigger man!'

'Bigger man?' laughed Donkey. '*Eee-aww, ee-aww!* Chance would be a fine thing! Toad is a tiny little squirt!'

Toad had had enough of being the butt of Donkey's jokes and he puffed out his chest in anger.

'OK, OK . . .' he croaked. 'You may be bigger but you definitely are not cleverer! I will race your big fat donkey hide and beat you hands down!'

The crowd that had gathered laughed and cheered.

'You tell him, Toad!'

'That's right, Toad, you can do it!'

'Yes, Toad! You are the cleverest!'

The animals in the crowd were always on the side of the underdog. They knew that Toad really didn't stand a chance of beating Donkey in a race, so they cheered him on to make him feel better. It also made *them* feel better to see Toad stand up for himself even though the odds were against him.

Toad and Donkey were always arguing about something and the rest of the animals found them very entertaining. Toad and Donkey rarely argued about anything in particular but somehow they managed to irritate each other with a look or a grunt or even a simple sigh. Today, though, the irritation was developing into a battle and neither of them was backing down.

'All right,' said Donkey, 'let's do it! The race is on!'

Toad had not expected Donkey to agree to the race so fast. He had hoped for more banter between them, to give him more time to see how he was going to outwit his long-time sparring partner.

'Today is not a good day for me,' said Toad quickly. 'I have things to do. Give me a few days to prepare.'

Donkey was in no mood for delaying tactics and was raring to go. He pawed the ground with his front hoof and made a cloud of dust, which almost choked the tiny Toad.

'I'm ready now! Let's do this!' he said, his nostrils flaring.

'We have to prepare!' said Toad, floundering. 'We can't just run when we don't even have a route and a finishing line! What kind of race would that be? Let's do this properly.'

'It's true,' said Wise Owl, who had woken from her sleep on the branch of a nearby tree. She had overheard the whole conversation. 'You can't have a race without a route and a finishing line. Why don't you start here on the savannah? Run up so, by the crooked tree. Run up the hill. When you reach the top of the hill, go straight, straight, straight until you reach the bend in the road. Follow the bend down the hill on the other side, then turn left by Bull's yard until you are back at the crooked tree. Then turn left and that will bring you back here.'

'OK,' said Toad.

'Fine with me,' agreed Donkey.

'Here are the rules,' said Wise Owl, because Wise Owl

knew about these things and she specialized in making rules. 'We'll mark five places on the route, each with a blue flag, the first by the crooked tree, the second at the top of the hill, the third on the bend in the road, the fourth on the other side at the bottom of the hill, the fifth on the gatepost of Bull's yard. At each of these five points, you have to call out to let us know you have got that far.'

'Right,' said Toad, 'let me get this right. I have to call out when I reach each of the five blue flags?'

'That's right,' said Wise Owl. 'That way we know how far you've reached.'

'When I reach each point I'll call out *croak-croak*,' said Toad.

'And I'll say *eee-aww, ee-aww*,' said Donkey.

'And the race will finish back here on the savannah, where we'll all be waiting,' said Wise Owl. 'Fowl and I will hold a big red ribbon for the finishing line and the first one to pass through the red ribbon is the winner!'

Toad and Donkey agreed that sounded like a good plan and the race was set for one o'clock that afternoon.

Wise Owl got her team together to mark the race route. Dog said he would be the one to give the order to start. Goat and his kids marked the five points in the race with blue flags. The rest of the animals wanted to make sure they didn't miss the excitement so they went home to make packed lunches ready to bring with them in the afternoon.

Once the time and place for the race were set, Donkey carried on working as normal, carrying bags of sand to his owner's home, as was his daily routine. He didn't see any point in resting and preparing for the race as he had no doubt in his mind that he would win.

Toad, on the other hand, began to worry about what he needed to do to outsmart Donkey. He decided he had better take a rest first so he would have lots of energy for the race. He went home to his wife and five children, but poor Toad couldn't rest. He couldn't stop thinking about how ridiculous he would look if he lost the race and how Donkey wouldn't ever let him live it down. He would feel so ashamed and didn't want to embarrass his family. He knew it would take him a long time to complete the route with his little legs. Toad decided to do some exercises to prepare. He flexed his tiny arms and legs over and over so he would be fit and ready.

'Come and eat!' Toad's wife said. 'You need a healthy meal. You'll need all your strength to win that race!' Toad's wife believed that Toad, even with his little legs, could beat Donkey in the race. Toad's five children all believed he could win too.

'You're going to win that race, Daddy!' they all croaked one after the other.

'You're going to win that race . . . You're going to win that race . . .'

The more they spoke about it, the more worried Toad

became. He didn't want to let them down. As Toad listened to all his children croaking, he heard how similar their voices sounded to his own and he suddenly had an idea.

'Come on,' he said, rallying his children together, 'I have a job for you.' Toad put his five children in his little bicycle cart. Soon he stopped at the crooked tree. He hid the first child behind a bush and he said to the child, 'I want you to wait here and listen for Mr Donkey. When you hear him cry out *eee-aww, ee-aww*, I want you to cry out *croak-croak*.' The child nodded obediently.

Toad rode to the next blue flag at the top of the hill and hid the second child behind a rock. He said to her, 'I want you to wait here and listen for Mr Donkey. When you hear him cry out *ee-aww, ee-aww*, I want you to cry out *croak-croak*.' The second child nodded obediently.

Then Toad rode his bicycle with his other three children to the next blue flags: the third on the bend in the road, the fourth on the other side at the bottom of the hill and the fifth on the gatepost of Bull's yard. At each flag he hid one of his children and gave each of them the same instructions: 'I want you to wait here and listen out for Mr Donkey. When you hear him cry out *eee-aww, ee-aww*, I want you to cry out *croak-croak*.' Each child nodded obediently.

Toad rode on his bicycle to the starting line of the race just in time, because by the time he had finished placing all his children at the marked points it was close to one o'clock. Donkey was already at the starting line waiting, looking strong and very eager to begin the race.

'What took you so long to get here?' he teased.

'Well I'm here now!' Toad said. 'And I'm ready for the race.'

Donkey's wife and children were sitting right in the front row, waiting for the race to begin, and each time Donkey boasted, 'I'm going to win! I'm going to win!' they cheered. 'Toad, you don't even have family to support you!' Donkey mocked. 'They have stayed at home because they don't want to be shamed!' he laughed.

'Not true!' said Toad's wife, pushing her way to the front of the crowd. 'The children are not here because they have chores to do, but they will be here later to celebrate when their father wins the race!'

Donkey laughed and laughed. '*Eee-aww, ee-aww!* You are full of jokes today!' Before Toad's wife could say anything more, Dog took his place and called for the race to begin.

'On your marks . . .' barked Dog, 'get ready . . . get set . . . GO!' and they were off. Donkey sped off straight away, leaving a cloud of dust behind him. Toad spluttered and coughed through the dust clouds, trying his best to keep up but, just as everyone had anticipated, Toad was way behind. Toad looked pitiful, scrambling in the dirt and bouncing as much as his little legs could carry him. Toad's wife applauded and cheered as if Toad was miles in front. The crowd watched them head off towards the forest and waited for their return.

Having created a good distance between himself and Toad, Donkey looked across the savannah and he thought he might as well stop to have a bite to eat. He knew there was no point in running flat out when Toad's little legs would take such a long time to catch up with him. After he had eaten, he looked back across the savannah in the direction of the starting line. He could see Toad away in the distance, struggling to keep up.

Donkey laughed. 'That Toad will never catch up with me. I may as well take a rest!' So Donkey got comfortable in the grass and fell asleep.

An hour later, Donkey woke up. He couldn't see Toad but he was sure that he was still way behind, so Donkey trotted over to the first blue flag by the crooked tree.

When Donkey reached the flag, he began to brag loudly, 'I'm going to beat that foolish Toad! How can that little thing think he is faster than me!' and remembering what Wise Owl had said, he called out, '*Eee-aww, ee-aww!*' to let everyone know he had reached the first marked point.

Toad's first child heard this and just as his father had told him he began to croak: '*Croak-croak, croak-croak!*'

Donkey could not believe his ears. How could Toad have got to the crooked tree so quickly when he had been so far behind? Maybe Donkey had slept for longer than he thought.

I must have spent too much time eating grass in the meadow and too much time sleeping, thought Donkey. *I had better get a move on!* And Donkey sped off as fast as his legs could carry him, this time only stopping for half a minute to drink some water along the way.

When Donkey got to the second blue flag at the top of the hill, he bragged loudly, 'I'm so much faster than that raggedy little Toad!' and he called out, *'Eee-aww, ee-aww!'* to let everyone know he had reached the second marked point. From behind the rock Toad's second child heard this and just as her father had told her she began to croak: *'Croak-croak, croak-croak!'*

Donkey was shocked. How could Toad have got to the top of the hill so quickly? 'I must run more quickly to the third blue flag,' said Donkey to himself, and he dashed off, trotting all the way without a break.

When he got to the bend in the road he laughed loudly, bragging, 'That little squirt Toad doesn't stand a chance of winning this race! I'm the champion! I'm the champion! *Eee-aww, ee-aww!'*

No sooner had he called out when Toad's third child began to croak from his hiding place: *'Croak-croak, croak-croak!'*

Donkey couldn't believe what he was hearing and he was very angry. How could Toad with his little legs be getting to the blue flags so quickly? Donkey was feeling tired now but there was no way he was going to let that little Toad beat him, so he ran off even faster than before to the bottom of the hill. But, alas, when Donkey reached the bottom of the hill, it was the same as before. As soon as Donkey let out his 'Eeee-aww' cry of victory, he heard what he thought was Toad's 'Croak-croak'. He felt defeated.

Still Donkey would not give up. Running flat out, he made it to the fifth blue flag at Bull's yard in quick time but he was completely exhausted. And yet again, when he called out 'Eee-aww, ee-aww!' his call was quickly followed by the 'Croak-croak' of Toad's fifth child. Donkey was so tired he leaned against Bull's gate and, before he knew it, he had fallen fast asleep.

Meanwhile, Toad was having a fine time. He had hidden himself behind a rock, halfway between the starting line and the first blue flag, and he had rested there, having exhausted himself on the bike ride. Now, fully rested, Toad had lots of energy. When he was good and ready, he got himself up and ran back to the place where they had started the race. This same place was now the finishing line. Wise Owl and Fowl were there, holding a big red ribbon for the winner to pass through. Toad ran and ran. He huffed and puffed to make it look like he was tired and had done the whole circuit. The crowd cheered when they saw him and, to everyone's surprise, Toad won the race!

Toad's victory party went on all afternoon and Toad's children soon joined the celebrations. There was no sign of Donkey. It was way into the evening, long after Toad's party had ended, when Donkey finally awoke from his snooze and, very embarrassed, he made his way back to the savannah. He was utterly ashamed of himself for losing a race against a tiny toad.

Donkey never heard the last of how Toad beat him, and never again did he brag about his speed . . .

Sookooyah

*This story is based on a mythical character
from the folklore of the Commonwealth of Dominica*

There was once a lonely old lady whose name was
Sandrine. Sandrine lived in a house way up on a hill,
far away from most of the people who lived in the small
village. She had once lived in the house with her husband,
Valentin. Valentin had built it himself. It was a simple
little building with hardly anything in it. There was just
one room where they slept and ate, and outside, at the side
of the house, was a small kitchen where they did their
cooking. Sandrine and Valentin would plant vegetables in
their garden and then cook them and eat them. Often

they would go to the river and fish, then bring home what they had caught and cook it up.

Occasionally, they would walk down to the village market where they would buy rice. It wasn't that they needed rice; in fact rice wasn't something they ate much of and they had lots of it already stored in their cupboard. But they enjoyed the walk and the chatter. Their life was simple and sweet and they were happy. They loved each other very, very much and they had vowed that only in death would they part.

The day Sandrine woke up to find that her husband had died was the saddest day of her life. They had spent so many years together and now she would spend the rest of her days alone.

At first Sandrine just stared out of her window, watching the sun rise and the sun set. She did not tend to the vegetables in her garden, she did not go fishing and she could not face going to the village market. Though she did not have much appetite her stomach rumbled and yearned for food. Luckily she had plenty of rice from the walks to the village market when Valentin was still alive.

Every day Sandrine would cook up a bowl of rice for her lunch. But now, being an old lady, her hands trembled so much that some of the rice would end up on the floor. Sandrine could not stand mess so her afternoons were spent picking up the small grains of rice that had fallen.

This would take a long time as she found it so difficult to bend her knees and straighten her back. Everything ached so much. Of course, Sandrine had a dustpan and sweeping brush and could have done the job so much quicker but she was so bored. It became a pastime of hers to count the grains of rice as she picked them up one by one, a habit she had become so used to that, even if she had wanted to, she didn't know how to break. Each day she would bend her aching body and reach out her arthritic fingers to pick up one tiny grain of rice at a time.

'One rice grain . . . two rice grain . . . three rice grain . . . four . . . Five rice grain . . . six rice grain . . . seven rice grain . . . more . . .' And so on.

When Sandrine had picked up all the rice she would take a nap, and after her nap she would sit by her window once again and watch the sky. She watched the birds spread their wings and fly and wished she could do the same. She wished her body didn't ache so much and wished she could wander around the streets like the wild animals. Instead all she could do these days was watch the sky and count rice grains.

One afternoon, while Sandrine was taking her nap, she heard someone call her name: 'Sandrine! Sandrine!'

When she opened her eyes, standing in front of her was a strange-looking creature. It was difficult to work out if what she was seeing was real or not as she was still half asleep and, besides, the room was dark on account of her closing the shutters to block out the sun. The creature she saw was about eight feet tall and looked like it was half man, half goat. The head was long like a goat's with two curly horns and a beard. The eyes were piercing red like a fire. The rest of the body looked like it belonged to a man, except for one thing: the creature had a long tail.

Sandrine screamed. 'Wha' you want?'

'I am Jab,' growled the strange creature. 'Don't be afraid. I have come to grant you a wish.'

Sandrine rubbed her eyes. She was sure she must be dreaming now as she had never seen a creature such as this before, especially one that proclaimed that he could grant wishes. In any case, what kind of wish could such an ugly creature grant her?

'Oh,' Sandrine said, not believing what she was seeing to be real. She closed her eyes again. 'Now let me sleep. I am an old lady and very tired.'

'I know that,' said Jab. 'I am here to grant you your greatest desire. Just tell me what would make you happy and I will give it to you!'

Still trying to get some sleep, Sandrine tried to make herself comfortable in her chair but the creature had disturbed her and the usual aches and pains were nagging at her joints again. For a moment she remembered the happiest times of her life and tears slipped from beneath her closed eyelids as she recalled good times spent with her beloved Valentin.

'Valentin,' she sighed, opening her eyes and looking at Jab. 'If you can grant a wish to make me happy, then bring Valentin back to me.'

'That I cannot do,' growled Jab. 'I cannot give life to the dead. Pick something else.'

'What kind of wish-giver are you, if you can't give me what I want!' snarled Sandrine. 'Valentin is the only thing that will make me truly happy. If you cannot give him to me then leave me and my aching body alone.'

'I can grant you *that* wish,' said Jab, taking a small bottle of oil from his bag. 'With this oil I can make your aches and pains go away.'

Sandrine opened her eyes again. Jab was grinning and holding a small bottle of oil in front of Sandrine's face.

'All you have to do is rub this oil on your skin,' Jab said 'and your pains will leave you.'

Sandrine was tired of the troublesome aches and pains. She reached her frail hand towards the bottle then stopped.

'What's the catch?' she asked. 'What do you want from me in return?'

'Nothing,' said Jab.

'I don't believe you,' said Sandrine, who had lived long

enough to know that there was a price for everything. 'Nothing's for nothing,' she said.

'Well, there is something . . .' said Jab. 'You have to follow my instructions and be back inside your house before daylight. If you are not inside your house before daylight as instructed then there is a price you must pay.'

'And what is the price?' asked Sandrine.

'If you don't get back inside your house before daylight then you will belong to me.'

Sandrine thought about what Jab had said. She was unsure what to do. She did not trust Jab at all but the thought of being free of her aches and pains, if only for a day, was too much for her to resist. She would make sure that she was back in her house before daylight.

'Give me the oil!' Sandrine said, and Jab passed the bottle to Sandrine.

Jab grinned. 'Now rub the oil all over your body until your skin is so soft and slippery that it drops off!'

'What? But I don't want my skin to drop off,' said Sandrine, thrusting the bottle back into Jab's hands.

'Trust me,' Jab said. 'You will only be out of your skin for a short while. Without your wrinkly old skin you will be able to travel out of your house with ease and enjoy roaming and, when you have finished roaming, you can come home and put your skin back on.'

Sandrine hesitated. This creature, Jab, did not look at all trustworthy. He looked like the sort of chap that would double-cross her, one that would say one thing and do something else. But she so wanted to take a trip out of her house and not to ache any more. Sandrine decided she was willing to take the chance to be rid of the tiresome aches and pains, if only for a short while.

'Turn around,' Sandrine said to Jab. He did as she asked. Sandrine quickly rubbed the oil all over her body until her skin was so slippery it came off like a coat. Then she looked around for somewhere to hide her wrinkly old skin, somewhere where Jab would not find it, should he want to trick her by keeping it from her.

Sandrine hid the wrinkled skin in her rice bowl for safe keeping and slid the bowl under her bed. When she bent down to do this, she could feel the effects of the oil already. She no longer felt any aches or pains in her body. All the pain that she had been feeling – in her knees, in her fingers, in her back – had gone away.

'This is amazing!' she said. 'I feel young again. Nothing hurts any more. I feel so light!'

'I told you!' said Jab. 'Now fly! Fly!' Jab breathed green smoke all over Sandrine. And, at once, Sandrine's feet left the ground and she floated out of the door.

'Hold on! Where am I going?' she called out, but Jab was nowhere to be seen to answer her cries. Sandrine flew up into the sky and all over the village, and she loved what she could see. From way up in the sky, she could see the river where she and Valentin had fished, and she could see the village market and the stallholders packing away their goods. She could see people going home from work and stray animals roaming the streets. As night fell Sandrine could feel her body lowering to the tops of houses where she hovered and, as people slept, she flew in and out of open windows, making people call out with fear! They were afraid when they saw her, because without her skin she looked so ugly. People couldn't tell if she was real or if they were dreaming.

'Keep away from me!' the people screamed. No one wanted Sandrine near them.

'It's only me,' Sandrine called, 'the old lady from the hilltop,' but they didn't seem to hear her. They ran from her as if she was going to do them harm.

Sandrine loved the fact that her body didn't hurt any more, she felt so light and free, but it made her feel sad that people were afraid of her. When the first glimmer of light peeped through the night sky Sandrine's flesh began to burn.

'Ouch! It's burning!' she said. 'It's nearly morning. I'd better get back to my skin!'

Sandrine quickly flew back home but Jab was a cunning devil. While Sandrine had been away enjoying herself he had mischievously sprinkled rice all over her doorstep, knowing she would not be able to resist picking up the grains.

When Sandrine arrived at her home she saw the rice sprinkled all over her doorstep and she was not pleased.

'Who's done this? Who's made a mess in front of my door?' Sandrine cried as she swooped down. 'This will never do! I've got to clean it up!' and Sandrine started to pick up the rice, grain by grain, as was her habit, counting each grain one at a time. She couldn't help herself.

'One rice grain . . . two rice grain . . . three rice grain . . . four . . . Five rice grain . . . six rice grain . . . seven rice grain . . . more . . .' And so on.

And as she counted the sun continued to come up. Jab watched as the skinless Sandrine counted the rice grains on her doorstep and he laughed.

'I catch you, Sandrine! Daylight has caught you without your skin! Now I own you! I will let you wear your wrinkled skin in the day but at night you will be transformed into a ball of fire. And every night you will be known as Sookooyah! And you will scare all those who walk these village streets alone,' said Jab.

Sandrine was distraught. She couldn't believe how foolish she had been to allow herself to be tricked by Jab, but she had made the deal with him and lost. There was no way out. She had to pay the price.

And every night, from that day on, Sandrine shed her skin and flew about, disturbing people in their dreams and scaring those who walked the village streets alone. She even grew to enjoy her new role, laughing at those she frightened. For it was more fun than sitting alone, with her aches and pains, feeling sorry for herself and counting rice grains.

To this day, when people walk alone through the villages late at night, it is claimed that Sookooyah, a ball of fire, can be seen flying through the darkness.

Coupay Cord-la

This story is based on a French Caribbean folk tale

I have heard it said that a long time ago there was a serious famine. All the animals were hungry and had to manage on any small scraps of food they could find. At this time, Brer Rabbit and Brer Wolf were both looking after their grannies, whom they loved very much.

'We really must do something or we're all going to starve,' said Brer Rabbit.

'We are all going to die,' said Brer Wolf, who had all but given up, 'and there's nothing we can do about it.'

But Brer Rabbit would not be beaten. He thought and thought and he came up with an idea.

'Brer Wolf,' said Brer Rabbit, 'I think I have the answer!'

Brer Wolf was feeling weak but he managed to lift up his head to listen to what Brer Rabbit had to say.

'And what is that?' he asked.

'These are desperate times,' said Brer Rabbit, 'and I don't want you to think badly of me, but . . . I think the best thing for us to do . . . well, it is to eat our grannies.'

Brer Wolf was in shock. 'Eat our grannies! Are you out of your mind? How can we eat our elders?'

'Well, my grannie has lived a long and happy life and, besides, she will be dead soon anyway so we may as well eat the meat from her bones!'

Brer Wolf thought that Brer Rabbit had gone mad. *How could anyone be so heartless as to eat their grannie?* he thought. Still, days went by without food and Brer Wolf grew hungrier and hungrier. When he looked at Brer Rabbit's grannie he started to imagine how tasty she would be on his plate.

When Brer Rabbit came back to Brer Wolf with the same suggestion, Brer Wolf licked his lips and said he thought maybe it wasn't a bad idea after all.

So Brer Wolf and Brer Rabbit devised a plan. They would make dinners out of their grannies. Both Brer Wolf and Brer Rabbit cried and cried about what they were going to do, but still they did not change their minds.

'I can see that you are very sad about the whole thing,' said Brer Rabbit to Brer Wolf, 'so, to make it easier for you,

I think it is only right that we eat your grannie f
you can get it out of the way.'

'That's very kind of you,' wept Brer Wolf.
with Brer Rabbit that his grannie should be cooked first
so he could get over the heartbreak as soon as possible.
They decided to cook her that very night.

So Brer Rabbit built a fire and put a big iron pot full of
water on it, and the weeping Brer Wolf captured his
grannie with a big net, as was the plan, and they put her in
the cooking pot.

That evening Brer Rabbit, Brer Rabbit's grannie and
Brer Wolf had a feast. The meat from Brer Wolf's grannie
lasted for weeks between them. But, once it had all
gone, Brer Wolf was hungry again.

'Now it's your turn,' said Brer Wolf. 'I'll make the
fire and prepare the pot of hot water while you go and
capture your grannie. Here's the net!' he said, handing
Brer Rabbit the same net he had used to capture his own
grannie.

With that, Brer Rabbit let out a big belly laugh. 'You
must be crazy if you think I am going to cook my grannie!'
he said. 'I only said that to trick you, so I could eat some
wolf meat!'

Brer Wolf was furious. How could he have been so
stupid as to believe that conniving rabbit? He had done a
terrible thing. He had eaten his own grannie! He was not

going to let Brer Rabbit get away with it. Brer Wolf had his eye on a tasty rabbit stew and Brer Rabbit's grannie was going to be the meat. Brer Wolf was going to make sure of that! He would sleep first and then hunt her down in the morning.

Brer Rabbit knew that Brer Wolf would want to get his own back, and so that night he secretly took his grannie out of her house and led her into the woods. Brer Rabbit found the tallest palm tree and he helped his grannie climb to the top. He gave her a basket with a cord tied to it.

'When I call out to you – "Grannie! Grannie! *Coupay cord-la!*" – you must drop the basket down and I will put food in it for you. Then you must pull on the cord and hoist up the basket. That way you'll get fed,' said Brer Rabbit.

The next morning Brer Wolf got up and went straight to Brer Rabbit's house.

'I've come for your grannie!' roared Brer Wolf.

'Too bad!' Brer Rabbit yelled back. 'She's not here!'

Brer Wolf tore through the house angrily, looking for Brer Rabbit's grannie, but he couldn't find her anywhere.

'Where are you hiding her?' he roared, but Brer Rabbit didn't give anything away. He just laughed.

Brer Wolf kept his watchful eye on Brer Rabbit but Brer Wolf was so weak and tired and hungry he fell asleep.

When he did so, Brer Rabbit slipped away and took a few scraps of food with him. He went into the woods and all the way to the tall palm tree.

When he got there he whispered up to his grannie, 'Grannie! Grannie! *Coupay cord-la!*' and when he did this, his grannie dropped the basket. Brer Rabbit put all the scraps of food he had found in the basket for her to eat. Then his grannie pulled on the cord and hoisted the basket up to the top of the palm tree. She ate the morsels of food that Brer Rabbit had brought for her and she drifted off to sleep.

'Goodnight, Grannie,' Brer Rabbit whispered gently and he went off back home.

But Brer Rabbit had not noticed that he was being watched. Brer Wolf had woken up, followed Brer Rabbit into the woods and he had seen everything. Once Brer Rabbit was out of sight, Brer Wolf went over to the tree and he called up, 'Grannie! Grannie! *Shoopay colla!*'

Brer Rabbit's grannie heard Brer Wolf call but she knew that it wasn't her grandson.

'That's not my grandson, Brer Rabbit!' she said to herself. 'He doesn't talk like that. He doesn't say *shoopay colla*!' So Brer Rabbit's grannie did not lower the basket to Brer Wolf. Brer Wolf was angry.

The next day Brer Rabbit returned to the tall palm tree in the woods and whispered up to his grannie, 'Grannie!

Grannie! *Coupay cord-la!*' When he did this, his grannie dropped the basket and Brer Rabbit put all the scraps of food he had found in the basket for her to eat. Then his grannie pulled on the cord and hoisted the basket up to the top of the palm tree as she had done before.

'Grandson, let me tell you a joke!' she called down to Brer Rabbit. 'Yesterday after you left someone came by and was hollering, "Grannie! Grannie! *Shoopay colla!*"'

Brer Rabbit and his grannie laughed and laughed. Brer Rabbit knew it must be Brer Wolf and told his grannie to be sure to listen carefully and to make sure she only responded to the correct call, which was, 'Grannie! Grannie! *Coupay cord-la!*'

Grannie told him she would make sure it was Brer Rabbit before she let down the basket.

While this was happening, Brer Wolf was hiding behind a tree and watching them while they laughed, and he got even angrier than before. Now he knew he had called incorrectly so he would make sure this time he got his words right. He waited for Brer Rabbit to leave and then, as he had done the night before, Brer Wolf went over to the tall palm tree and hollered, 'Grannie! Grannie! *Coupay cord-la!*'

Brer Rabbit's grannie was suspicious straight away. Brer Wolf did not whisper in a light voice as Brer Rabbit had done.

'My grandson doesn't sound like that!' said Brer Rabbit's

grannie to herself. 'My grandson speaks in a light whisper. He doesn't holler so loudly. This must be an imposter!' And she did not let down her basket. Brer Wolf was vexed. He went home hungry once again.

The next day Brer Rabbit returned to the tall palm tree in the woods with some scraps of food and he whispered gently up to his grannie, 'Grannie! Grannie! *Coupay cord-la!*' When he did this, his grannie dropped the basket and once again he put all the scraps of food he had found in the basket for her to eat. Then his grannie pulled on the cord and hoisted the basket up to the top of the palm tree as she had done before.

'Grandson, let me tell you a joke!' she called down to Brer Rabbit. 'Yesterday after you left someone came by and was hollering, "Grannie! Grannie! *Coupay cord-la!*" in a loud fierce voice. I knew it wasn't you because when you call me, you call in a gentle whisper!'

Brer Rabbit and his grannie laughed and laughed. Brer Rabbit knew it must be Brer Wolf and told his grannie to be sure to listen carefully next time she heard him call and to make sure she only responded to the correct call, which was Brer Rabbit saying, 'Grannie! Grannie! *Coupay cord-la!*' in a gentle whisper.

Once again, Grannie told him she would make sure it was Brer Rabbit calling before she let down the basket.

*

As they spoke, Brer Wolf was hiding behind a tree just as before and watching them while they laughed. He got even angrier than before. Now he knew he had to say the words in a gentle whisper, he would make sure this time he got it right. Brer Wolf waited for Brer Rabbit to leave and then, as he had done before, Brer Wolf went over to the tall palm tree. This time, he tried to speak in a gentle whisper: 'Grannie! Grannie! *Coupay cord-la!*' but the words came out rough and loud. He began to cough and splutter as he tried to make his voice sound softer.

'Grannie! Grannie!' he screeched. *'Coupay cord-la!'* But try as he might Brer Wolf's voice would not whisper. It just barked loud and fierce.

'I know you are not my grandson!' called Brer Rabbit's grannie. 'My grandson talks softly. Your voice is too harsh!' Having been found out, Brer Wolf ran away from the woods to think about what to do next.

Brer Wolf was angry. He stomped around, annoyed at how Brer Rabbit had got the better of him. He was determined to get his own back, whatever the cost! He had to find a way to soften his voice so that Brer Rabbit's grannie would think it was Brer Rabbit calling her.

Now Brer Rabbit was smart and knew that Brer Wolf would be trying all kinds of ways to fool his grannie, so he passed by Brer Wolf's home on purpose, singing a song.

'*The blacksmith alone can make my voice soft.*
There lies my secret!'

And he sang it over and over again.

'*The blacksmith alone can make my voice soft.*
There lies my secret!'

Brer Rabbit knew that the only thing that the blacksmith did to him whenever he went there was to try to keep him away by beating him with his red hot poker. But Brer Wolf didn't know this and his ears stood up immediately when he heard Brer Rabbit's song.

'The blacksmith holds the secret to Brer Rabbit's soft voice!' he said to himself. He made his way to the blacksmith's straight away.

The blacksmith was busy at his hot stove heating up a metal poker when Brer Wolf arrived. The blacksmith put the metal poker in the fire and the metal hissed a whisper. Brer Wolf heard the hissing whisper and thought that the hot poker must be what Brer Rabbit used to get his soft voice.

'Give me some of that!' Brer Wolf shouted to the blacksmith. The blacksmith was so startled when he heard Brer Wolf that he rammed the poker down Wolf's big open mouth.

'Whoooooooaaaa!' Brer Wolf cried as the hot metal burned his throat.

Brer Rabbit was watching and he laughed so much he almost split his sides.

Brer Wolf felt sorry for himself. He went straight to bed and howled all night. The next morning, when he woke up, his throat was so sore he could hardly speak. In fact, every word he said sounded like a whisper!

'Now's my chance. I'll show that Brer Rabbit!' Brer Wolf said to himself, and he made his way back to the palm tree in the woods where Brer Rabbit had hidden his grannie. When he got there he whispered, 'Grannie! Grannie! *Coupay cord-la!*'

Brer Rabbit's grannie heard the call and, believing it to be her grandson bringing her food, she lowered the basket down.

When the basket reached the bottom of the tree Brer Wolf climbed inside and waited for Brer Rabbit's grannie to pull on the cord and hoist the basket back up to the top of the palm tree, as he had seen her do.

Brer Rabbit's grannie felt the heavy weight of the basket and smiled. 'My grandson loves me so much!' she said to herself. 'He has brought me plenty of food today. The basket is much heavier than usual.' Brer Rabbit's grannie could hardly lift the weight of the basket as she slowly pulled on the cord. She was sweating because the basket was so heavy. Still, she pulled as hard as she could, looking forward to her feast.

As she pulled on the cord, Brer Rabbit was making his

way through the woods with some scraps of food. When he got to the clearing he could see his grannie's palm tree and he could see the basket slowly being hoisted to the top, with Brer Wolf inside it!

Brer Rabbit ran as fast as he could through the woods. When he got to the palm tree the basket was almost at the top of the tree.

'Grannie! Grannie! *Coupay cord-la!*' Brer Rabbit called and, on hearing Brer Rabbit's voice, Brer Rabbit's grannie dropped the basket with Brer Wolf in it, smashing him to the ground. Brer Wolf never troubled Brer Rabbit's grannie again.

The Man and his Servant

*This story is based on a folk tale from the
Commonwealth of Dominica*

Long ago, when stories were told in Dominica, it was
common for the storyteller to call out 'Eh Kwik!' and,
in response, those who were listening would call back
'Eh Kwak!'

Eh Kwik!

Eh Kwak!

There was once a very rich old man. His name was
Monsieur Jacques.

Eh Kwik!

Eh Kwak!

Monsieur Jacques lived in a big house at the top of a hill

with his servant, Daniel. He had no wife or family. Daniel had worked for Monsieur Jacques for many years and he was a loyal servant. Over the years they had become good friends and folks said that, when the old man died, more than likely he would leave a respectable sum of money to Daniel.

Monsieur Jacques wasn't a bad employer and Daniel enjoyed working for him. Daniel would go beyond his regular duties to provide good service for Monsieur Jacques.

Eh Kwik!

Eh Kwak!

When Daniel cooked for Monsieur Jacques he would make sure he cooked with only the best meat and vegetables.

When he cleaned Monsieur Jacques' home, Daniel would make sure he cleaned to perfection until there was not a speck of dirt in sight.

After cooking and cleaning, Daniel would fix up the yard, plant vegetables and run errands for Monsieur Jacques. He would even nurse him when he was sick.

Daniel did so much for Monsieur Jacques that you would often hear gossipers in the village laugh and say, 'The only thing Daniel doesn't do for that man is die for him!'

Eh Kwik!

Eh Kwak!

Though Daniel heard their gossiping, he didn't pay any attention to their idle chit-chat. Daniel was a kind man and Monsieur Jacques had been good to him. Monsieur Jacques had given him work when he had had no money and he had given him somewhere to live too. Daniel was very grateful to him.

One day Monsieur Jacques sent Daniel into town on some errands. He asked him to go to the baker's shop to buy some bread, to go to the tailor's to pick up his suit, and as he wasn't feeling well he asked Daniel to pass by the doctor's to pick up his pills. Daniel gladly went on his way.

Eh Kwik!

Eh Kwak!

As Daniel was walking down the road, he could feel somebody watching him, which was strange as there didn't seem to be anybody about. This in turn was strange, as there was usually somebody about in the street at ten o'clock in the morning. Not today. Today there wasn't a soul to be seen.

Still, the feeling of being watched didn't go away. Daniel could sense eyes staring into him and it made the hairs stand up on the back of his neck. He looked over his shoulder and all around to see if he could see anyone. After doing this for some time, Daniel called out, 'Who is there?'

Nobody answered.

Eh Kwik!

Eh Kwak!

Daniel carried on walking. This time he walked a little faster, sometimes missing his footing and almost falling over in his haste. All the time he was looking over his shoulder to see if anyone was there. There was never anyone or anything around. Daniel felt uneasy, and to try make himself less scared Daniel began to sing his list to himself.

> *'A loaf of bread from the baker,*
> *Pick up the suit from the tailor*
> *And collect the pills from the doctor.'*

He sang it over and over again.

> *'A loaf of bread from the baker,*
> *Pick up the suit from the tailor*
> *And collect the pills from the doctor.'*

This made him feel a little better, but still the feeling of being watched would not go away.

Then suddenly, as Daniel walked quickly along, a big black shadow appeared from nowhere and darkened his path.

Eh Kwik!

Eh Kwak!

'Who are you? Why are you following me?' Daniel asked the shadow in fright.

There was no answer.

Daniel began to walk even more quickly, shouting behind him as he walked, 'Go away! Go away!' but still the shadow stayed with him, an uninvited companion. The shadow grew bigger and bigger and followed Daniel all the way to the baker's shop.

Eh Kwik!

Eh Kwak!

Once inside the baker's shop, breathless, Daniel crouched in front of the counter and tried to peep out of the window to see who or what it was following him that could cast a shadow so large.

'What's wrong with you?' the baker asked. He was used to Daniel buying bread for Monsieur Jacques but he had never seen the man behave in such a way before. 'Have you come to buy Monsieur Jacques his bread or have you just come to hide inside my shop?'

Daniel tried to explain. 'I am being followed,' he said. 'On my way here, I felt like I was being watched. Then a big black shadow started hanging around me and followed me all the way here! I'm just trying to see what it is.'

'You say a big black shadow followed you all the way here?' said the baker. He peered out of his window but couldn't see anything. The big black shadow had gone. 'I can't see anything out there. Perhaps you imagined it? You're probably overtired and hallucinating. That Monsieur Jacques sure works you hard!'

'It was there!' Daniel insisted. 'It followed me all the way here.'

The baker laughed. Embarrassed, Daniel bought the bread he had been sent to pick up and ran quickly out of the shop. Maybe the baker was right and he was so tired that he was seeing things.

Daniel walked towards the tailor's shop. He wanted to finish his tasks quickly so that he could get home and rest as soon as possible.

Eh Kwik!

Eh Kwak!

As he hurriedly made his way to the tailor's shop, once again he could feel someone watching him. Each time he turned around to see who it was there was no one there. Then, just as before, the big shadow returned.

'I don't know who you are or what you want!' said Daniel. 'But *please* leave me alone!'

The big black shadow would not leave him alone. It followed Daniel wherever he went.

'Go away! Go away!' Daniel shouted.

The shadow wouldn't go away. Daniel became more and more frightened. He walked more quickly than ever but he couldn't escape the shadow.

Once again, to try to make himself feel less scared, Daniel began to sing.

'I have the bread from the baker,'

he sang, trembling.

> *'Now the suit from the tailor*
> *Then the pills from the doctor.'*

He sang his song over and over again.

> *'I have the bread from the baker,*
> *Now the suit from the tailor*
> *Then the pills from the doctor.'*

And all along the way, the big black shadow followed Daniel to the tailor's shop.

Eh Kwik!

Eh Kwak!

Daniel was so frightened he almost broke the tailor's door down to get inside the shop.

'Let me in! Let me in!' he shouted, banging on the door. The tailor often locked his shop door as he worked on his suits in the back room. Sometimes he would get carried away with his tailoring and would forget all about the front of his shop, so he had a sign on the door that read KNOCK IF YOU WANT SOMETHING IN MY SHOP.

'Be careful!' said the tailor, as he opened the door for Daniel. 'I hear you. You don't have to knock so hard! That door cost me a lot of money!'

'I'm sorry,' Daniel said. 'It's just that I'm having a

peculiar day. I set off this morning from Monsieur Jacques' house to get some bread and all the way to the baker's shop it felt like someone was watching me. A big black shadow followed me all the way to the baker's shop and now it has followed me all the way here!'

The tailor looked out of his shop window immediately to see if he could see the black shadow. There was nothing there.

'You say a big black shadow followed you all the way here?' said the tailor. 'I can't see anything out there. Perhaps you imagined it. You're probably tired and hallucinating. That Monsieur Jacques sure works you hard!'

Daniel sighed. Maybe the baker and the tailor were right. Maybe all the hard work he did for Monsieur Jacques had made him so tired he was seeing things.

'Maybe you're right,' Daniel said, peeking out of the window. And just as when he had looked out of the baker's window, there was nothing there.

'Here's Monsieur Jacques's suit,' said the tailor, 'exactly how he wanted it, made to his measurements.' Daniel thanked the tailor and paid for the suit. Then he left.

Eh Kwik!

Eh Kwak!

As Daniel stepped outside the tailor's shop he once again could feel that he was being watched. Just as before, the big shadow that had been following him returned.

Daniel didn't know what to do. He still had Monsieur

Jacques' pills to get from the doctor's and the doctor lived on the other side of town. It was such a long way to go with a big black shadow following him. Daniel was very afraid. What could the big black shadow be and what could it possibly want?

Immediately Daniel began to sing to try and get rid of his fear.

> *'I have the bread from the baker,*
> *And the suit from the tailor,*
> *Now the pills from the doctor.'*

Daniel sang his song over and over again.

> *'I have the bread from the baker,*
> *And the suit from the tailor,*
> *Now the pills from the doctor.'*

He sang his song louder and louder.

> *'I HAVE THE BREAD FROM THE BAKER,*
> *AND THE SUIT FROM THE TAILOR,*
> *NOW THE PILLS FROM THE DOCTOR!'*

all the way along.
Eh Kwik!
Eh Kwak!

As Daniel walked and sang, the sun began to go down. As it got darker, the big shadow eventually disappeared. Daniel was relieved. At last he was free of the big black shadow! He continued on his long journey to the doctor's house.

But although Daniel was free of the big shadow, he could still feel the piercing eyes of something or someone watching him. With all the courage he could find, Daniel turned around and shouted:

'IF YOU CANNOT TELL ME WHAT YOU WANT THEN LEAVE ME ALONE!'

Then, from out of the blackness, two big green eyes glowed. They were staring right at him. As soon as Daniel saw the green eyes, he knew exactly who it was following him.

Those big green eyes belonged to only one being ... and that was Death!

'Oh no!' screamed Daniel. 'If Death is following me, that can only mean one thing! He has come to take me!'

Daniel began to run. Everyone in the community knew that when it was your time to die the mysterious Death would come personally to collect you. Though no one alive had met him, it was commonly known that Death had piercing green eyes.

Daniel ran and ran. He was not ready to die yet! He had so much to do. He was hoping that one day he might find a wife and raise a family. He hadn't done that yet! All he had done with his life so far was work for Monsieur Jacques. No, he was not ready to die! So Daniel ran and ran and ran until he finally got back to Monsieur Jacques' house.

Eh Kwik!

Eh Kwak!

When he arrived, Monsieur Jacques was surprised to see him back so early. He didn't notice how pale and petrified Daniel looked. All he seemed to care about was whether Daniel had completed his tasks.

'Did you get my bread?' he asked.

'Yes, I have your bread,' Daniel said, his heart pounding. He checked the window to see if Death had followed him.

'Good, good,' said Monsieur Jacques. 'And my suit? Did you collect my suit?'

'Yes, I have your suit,' said Daniel, handing it over.

'And my pills? Did you get my pills?'

Daniel suddenly remembered that he had not managed to collect the pills.

'Sorry, Monsieur Jacques, but . . .' and before Daniel could explain what had happened Monsieur Jacques was pushing him out of the door.

'You must go and get them immediately!' he said. 'I am not feeling good at all.'

'I can't!' Daniel screamed. 'A terrible thing has happened. When I left you to go and get the errands I felt like I was being watched! And then a big black shadow followed me all the way to the baker's, and then to the tailor's – and then

I noticed that the shadow had big green eyes and was none other than Death! What am I to do? I am not ready to die yet!'

Monsieur Jacques was saddened by what he had heard. He didn't want Daniel to die either. Daniel had been a loyal servant and his most trusted friend for many years.

'Here's what we shall do,' said Monsieur Jacques, looking out of the window to make sure Death was not waiting outside. 'You must get away from here. I will give you some money so you can start a new life in a new city far away where Death cannot find you. You mustn't worry, Daniel. Pack some things and go!'

Daniel was so afraid he couldn't concentrate, so Monsieur Jacques packed up his things and a lot of money for his servant and put them in a bag. Monsieur Jacques made sandwiches for Daniel out of the bread Daniel had got from the baker's and he even gave Daniel the smart suit that Daniel had collected for him from the tailor's. It fitted Daniel well and made him look like a fine gentleman.

Daniel got excited. He thanked Monsieur Jacques for his generosity. He had enough money to start a new life now. Daniel would settle down and raise a family of his own. He was very happy.

Daniel slipped out of the back door and ran as fast as he could away from Monsieur Jacques' house.

Eh Kwik!

Eh Kwak!

When he had gone, Monsieur Jacques sat alone in his house and wondered how he would manage without his loyal servant and trusted friend. He was thinking about how lonely he was going to be when there was a loud knock at the door.

Monsieur Jacques looked out of his window and saw the piercing green eyes of Death looking back at him. Death's eyes were cold and without emotion. Death knocked on the door again, even louder than before. Monsieur Jacques refused to open the door.

'You can knock as loudly as you like!' said Monsieur Jacques. His heart was broken having lost his good friend and as he spoke a sharp pain darted across his chest.

Monsieur Jacques reached for his pills but, of course, his pill bottle was empty.

Death knocked louder and louder.

'Daniel has gone! You won't find him here!' Monsieur Jacques called weakly.

And Death burst through the door, his foreboding presence filling the room .

'The truth is,' said Death in a cold echoing voice, 'I never came for Daniel. I came for you.'

And Death let out a bellowing laugh as Monsieur Jacques took his last breath and died . . .

Eh Kwik.

Eh Kwak.

Brer Anansi and Brer Snake

This story is based on a folk tale from Tobago

Word had got round in the animal village that a famine was coming. Wise Owl, who knew everything, announced it one evening.

All the animals looked worried. All, that is, except for Brer Anansi. He had decided long ago that there was no sense worrying about anything since he was always able to get himself out of a tight spot.

As all of the animals gathered to think up a plan, Brer Anansi just relaxed in the sun and waited for them to finish talking. When they had finished, Brer Anansi caught up to Brer Snake.

'So what has been decided?' he asked.

Brer Snake told him. 'Everyone has decided to work the land. If we all plant lots of vegetables then there will be plenty of food for everyone, come harvest time.'

Brer Anansi laughed. 'I'm not working the land!' he said. 'You all can do the work and when you're done I'll just steal what you've planted. No one can stop me!'

Brer Snake didn't like what he heard. He told all the animals in the village what Brer Anansi planned to do, so everyone put up fences and made sure they were waiting to pounce on Anansi should he attempt to steal from them.

When the time came for harvest, they made sure Brer Anansi could not get to their crops.

This made Brer Anansi angry.

'I'm so hungry!' he said to Brer Snake one day. 'I have tried to steal food but everyone has put up fences around their crop and I can't sneak in and get any! What am I to do?'

'That's your own fault,' said Brer Snake. 'You should have grown your own vegetables like the rest of us.'

'Oh no!' said Brer Anansi. 'And now it's too late! I am going to starve.'

'Well,' said Brer Snake, who felt sorry for him now, 'I have a garden full of vegetables. I can give you some potatoes, okras, yams and plantains. But I want something in return.'

'Oh, what's that?' asked Brer Anansi.

'In return,' said Brer Snake, 'I want to lash you with my long tail.'

Brer Anansi thought about Brer Snake's proposal and he agreed to take a lashing from Brer Snake's tail for some food.

Brer Snake handed over the potatoes, okras, yams and plantains.

'Here, take the vegetables and enjoy your supper. I will come to your home at midnight tonight and I will give you the lashing with my tail,' said Brer Snake.

Brer Anansi agreed and took the vegetables home to cook. He already had a plan in his mind of how to avoid Brer Snake's lashing, so he wasn't worried.

Once home, Brer Anansi put all the vegetables in a big pot of water on his stove. Whilst he waited for it to cook he sang out loudly so any animals in the street could hear:

> *I am Brer Anansi,*
> *I am Brer Anansi.*
> *Come and join me –*
> *I have a big feast tonight!'*

Brer Goat was passing by and he heard Brer Anansi singing.

'What's that you say, Brer Anansi? You're having a feast?'

'Yes,' said Brer Anansi. 'I have okras and yams and plantains and potatoes . . .'

Well, Brer Goat likes his food and eats almost anything, so he wasn't about to let that offer pass him by. He went into Brer Anansi's home to enjoy the feast that he had prepared. There was more than enough food for both of them to eat and when Brer Goat's belly was full he snuggled up and fell asleep, just as Brer Anansi had hoped.

At midnight there was a loud knock on the door.

'Brer Goat!' shouted Brer Anansi. 'Wake up! Someone is at the door. Please could you answer it for me?'

Brer Goat woke up out of his sleep and went to the door. As he opened the door, Brer Snake gave him one lash with his tail and knocked Brer Goat over in one blow. Then, without looking back to see who it was that he had lashed, Brer Snake went on his way, satisfied that he had received full payment for the vegetables.

When Brer Snake had gone, Brer Anansi got up and saw Brer Goat lying dead on the ground and he laughed. 'I missed Snake's lashing and I get fresh meat!' he said. Then he cleaned up the goat meat and cut it up and put it in the pot with some seasoning, ready to make another big feast for the next day. The only trouble was, there were no vegetables left to eat the goat stew with. Brer Anansi decided he would go and see Brer Snake in the morning and ask him for some more vegetables.

Brer Anansi got up bright and early the next day and went to visit Brer Snake.

'Brer Snake, I have eaten all the vegetables you gave me and now I am hungry again! Please could I have some more?'

Brer Snake was shocked to see Brer Anansi after the lashing he had thought he had given him.

'You are very tough, Brer Anansi! I thought that lashing I gave you last night would have finished you off.'

'The good food you gave me made me tough!' laughed Brer Anansi. 'So what do you say? Do you have any more vegetables for me?'

'I can give you some green bananas and plantains and some yams,' said Brer Snake. 'But the deal is the same as before. In return, I want to lash you with my long tail.'

Brer Anansi smiled. 'That's fine with me,' he said. So Brer Snake handed over the green bananas, plantains and yams.

'Here, take the vegetables and enjoy your supper. I will come to your home at midnight again tonight and I will give you the lashing with my tail,' said Brer Snake.

Brer Anansi agreed and took the vegetables home to cook. He was wondering who he could catch to take Brer Snake's lashings for him.

When he got home, Brer Anansi put all the vegetables in a big pot of water on his stove. When they were cooked he served them together with the stewed goat. What a feast Brer Anansi had! He was enjoying it so much he almost forgot his plan. Then he remembered he needed to catch somebody else to collect Brer Snake's lashing. So, as before Brer Anansi sang out loudly so that any animals passing in the street could hear:

> *'I am Brer Anansi,*
> *I am Brer Anansi.*
> *Come and join me –*
> *I have a big feast tonight!'*

Brer Hog was passing by and he heard Brer Anansi singing.

'A feast, Brer Anansi?' said Brer Hog.

'Yes,' said Brer Anansi. 'I have green bananas, plantains and yams and a little goat meat. Come and join me!' He ushered Brer Hog into his home.

Well, Brer Hog eats almost anything, and he enjoyed all the food that Brer Anansi had prepared. Brer Hog ate until his belly was full and then, as Brer Goat had done before him, Brer Hog snuggled up and fell asleep.

Once again, at midnight, there was a knock on the door.

'Brer Hog!' shouted Brer Anansi. 'Wake up! Someone is at the door. Please could you answer it for me?'

Brer Hog woke up out of his sleep and went to the door. As he opened the door, Brer Snake gave him one lash with his tail and knocked Brer Hog over in one blow. Then, without even looking back, Brer Snake went on his way, satisfied that he had lashed Brer Anansi and received full payment for the vegetables he had given to him.

When Brer Snake had gone, Brer Anansi got up and saw Brer Hog lying dead on the ground. He laughed. 'I missed Snake's lashing and I get fresh meat!' he said. He cleaned up the hog meat, cut it up and put it in the pot with some seasoning, ready to make another big feast for the next day. The only trouble was, there were no vegetables left to eat the stew with. Brer Anansi decided that he would go and see Brer Snake in the morning and ask him yet again to give him more vegetables.

So the next morning, Brer Anansi got up bright and early and went to visit Brer Snake. Brer Snake was shocked to see Brer Anansi after having giving him two lashings with his tail.

'I was wondering if you could spare some more vegetables?' Brer Anansi said.

'Well,' said Brer Snake, ' I am shocked to see you still alive but since you are still going strong I suppose I could give you some callaloo and potatoes.'

'Is that all?' asked Brer Anansi greedily.

'Yes, that is all,' said Brer Snake. 'And the deal is the same as before. I will come at midnight and give you a lashing with my tail as payment.'

Brer Anansi agreed and he took the callaloo and the potatoes from Brer Snake and went home.

Once home, Brer Anansi put all the vegetables in a big pot of water on his stove. When the vegetables were cooked he served them together with the stewed hog. What a feast Brer Anansi had! The stewed hog and the vegetables were delicious. Brer Anansi looked outside to see if anyone was passing but there was no one in sight. Brer Anansi began to sing out loudly to see if he could attract anyone's attention:

> *'I am Brer Anansi,*
> *I am Brer Anansi.*
> *Come and join me –*
> *I have a big feast tonight!'*

But word must have got round because no one was coming to share Brer Anansi's feast with him tonight. He sang out loudly again:

> *'I am Brer Anansi,*
> *I am Brer Anansi.*
> *Come and join me –*
> *I have a big feast tonight!'*

But still no one was enticed by Brer Anansi's song or the sweet smell of his food. Brer Anansi began to worry. In a couple of hours it would be midnight and Brer Snake would be coming to give out his nightly lashing with his tail. What was he going to do? Brer Anansi had an idea. He started to drum and dance and sing:

'Big, big party tonight!
Big, big party tonight!
Big, big party tonight,
All welcome!'

As Brer Anansi sang and danced and played his drum, Brer Armadillo came up to him. Now Brer Armadillo does not care too much for cooked food as he lives on rotten wood and worms, but he does like a good party.

'I'll come to your party!' called Brer Armadillo, and he danced into Brer Anansi's home. Brer Armadillo didn't eat any of the food that Brer Anansi had but he enjoyed joining in with all the singing and the dancing. Brer Anansi kept him entertained all evening, and Brer Armadillo danced and danced until he was exhausted. Finally Brer Armadillo asked Brer Anansi if he could stay the night. When Brer Anansi said that he could, Brer Armadillo went and dug a hole by the door and he fell asleep there.

At midnight, just as Brer Anansi expected, there was a knock on the door.

'Brer Armadillo!' called Brer Anansi. 'Wake up! Someone is at the door! Please could you answer the door for me?'

Brer Armadillo barely moved. Instead he just carried on sleeping.

The knocking on the door got louder.

'Brer Armadillo!' shouted Brer Anansi. 'Wake up, I tell you! There's somebody at the door!'

'What business is it of mine?' asked Brer Armadillo, stirring in his sleep.

'I want you to open the door for me!' Brer Anansi called.

But Brer Armadillo said, 'This is not my house, it's yours!'

'But I am sick in bed, I have a fever!' Brer Anansi said.

'Even so, it is for *you* to open the door for your guests, not me. I'm not going to open someone else's door!' said Brer Armadillo.

Well, Brer Snake was getting angry. He had made a deal with Brer Anansi and he wanted to make sure that he lashed Anansi with his tail, as they had agreed. He knocked on the door harder and harder until he knocked so hard he knocked the door down with his tail.

Brer Anansi was frightened now. He tried to hide himself under his furniture. He put the sofa and table and chair on top of himself, but Brer Snake was so angry he lashed at the furniture and knocked it all away. And, at last, he lashed Brer Anansi.

From that day on, Brer Anansi vowed he would stop begging and stealing, and instead work hard for himself.

The Elf-Stone

This story is based on a folk tale from the
Dominican Republic

There was once a young woman called Maria. She
loved a man named Juan very much. Maria worked as
a cook in the big house where Juan lived, and every day
she would see him and dream about marrying him. But
Juan was so handsome and rich, and Maria was so plain
and poor, and all the rich women in the village were
always parading themselves in front of Juan wearing
their fancy gowns, expensive jewellery and extravagant
hairstyles. How could Maria compete with them? She
only had one dress to wear and it was full of holes. Maria
couldn't afford any jewellery and her hair was wild and

free. She knew Juan would eventually choose one of the rich ladies to marry and she knew that when he did it would break her heart.

Still, Juan always greeted Maria with a smile when she turned up for work and it made her feel like she was the most beautiful woman in the world. She couldn't help but continue to dream about the impossible.

One day Maria was walking home from work when an old woman caught up and walked with her.

'Don't be sad,' said the woman.

'I'm not sad!' said Maria. 'Why should I be?'

'Yes you are,' said the woman. 'I can see it in your eyes.'

It was true that Maria did have a sadness in her eyes, because of the longing she had for Juan.

'You have a longing,' said the woman. 'But don't worry. Your dream to marry Juan can come true!'

Maria was shocked. She had not shared her dream of marrying Juan with anyone.

'How do you know about my dream of marrying Juan?' Maria asked.

'I know everything,' said the woman. 'I have watched you and I see how you look at him.'

'But I've never seen you before,' said Maria.

'I work at the big house too,' said the woman. 'I pick up the laundry every Friday at Juan's house, I wash the family's clothes in the river, and then I bring back the clothes to the house all clean and ironed on a Monday.'

Maria felt ashamed that she had never noticed the woman before.

'I have been watching you for some time,' said the woman, 'but you will not have noticed me because you only have eyes for Juan. Anything else that is happening around you goes unnoticed.'

Maria felt embarrassed. She wondered who else had noticed her looking at Juan and a wave of fear suddenly hit her as she wondered if Juan too knew how she felt about him.

'Well, it's just a dream,' said Maria. 'Nothing can ever come of it. It's just a dream.'

'Don't you say that,' said the woman, 'for I can help make your dream come true. But if I help you marry Juan it will cost you a lot of money.'

Maria laughed. 'If only . . .' she said.

'It's up to you,' said the woman. 'If you want him I can help you, but if you don't . . . It's up to you.'

Maria thought for a moment. The woman was very convincing. If she could actually make Maria's dream a reality, it would be truly amazing.

'I don't have any money,' said Maria, 'so even if you can help me, I wouldn't be able to pay you.'

'Once you are married to Juan, you will be rich too,' said the woman. 'You can pay me when you're married.'

Maria realized she had nothing to lose. If the woman

failed to get Juan to marry Maria then she would not have to pay her. The deal seemed too good to be true.

'What's the catch?' she asked.

'No catch!' said the woman sweetly.

Maria loved Juan so much. If this woman could help her then maybe it would be worth the risk.

'Yes,' said Maria. 'Help me to marry Juan.'

'Now you must listen very carefully to my instructions,' said the woman, 'and you must follow them completely.'

'Yes,' said Maria. 'Just tell me what I must do.'

'You must get an elf-stone,' said the woman.

'An elf-stone? What's an elf-stone?' asked Maria.

'It's a very special stone that has the powers to give you what you wish for.'

'Where will I get one from? What does it look like?' asked Maria.

'You must go to the small cave by the stream in the middle of the forest to get it. The elf-stone is in the shape of a man,' said the woman. 'When you go to the cave, be sure to take someone with you.'

'I'll call my brother to go with me,' said Maria.

The woman looked concerned. 'I'm afraid that's not allowed. Men are not allowed to go along. Your companion must be female.'

'But I don't have any sisters and my mother is dead!' said Maria.

'Then I will go with you,' said the woman. Maria had no reason to disagree.

'To complete the spell, you must bring with you a photograph of Juan,' said the woman. 'I will place the elf-stone on top of the picture and put them on the ground at the main crossroads when it is raining and the sun is shining, just as a rainbow fills the sky. After I have cast my spell, I will bury the picture and the elf-stone in the earth.'

'And then will that be it? Will I marry Juan?' asked Maria.

'Most certainly,' the woman said. 'Meet me at the cemetery gate with the photograph of Juan tomorrow evening at six o'clock.'

Maria agreed to meet the woman at the cemetery gate at six o'clock the next day.

Maria went home feeling very excited. Could what the woman have said to her be true? If Maria followed all the instructions, would Juan really become her husband?

The next day, when Maria went to work at the big house as usual, she felt very happy. When Juan passed her and smiled in his usual way, though she was just a poor girl in rags, once again she felt like the most beautiful girl in the world. She hoped desperately that the woman's spell with the elf-stone would work.

There were so many photographs of Juan around the house. It would be easy to take one without it being missed, so Maria chose a photograph of Juan on a fine black horse from the large wooden dresser in the main room of the house. When she had finished her work and was about to leave, she carefully put the photograph of Juan in her bag and hurried to meet the woman at the cemetery gate as she had agreed.

'I have the photograph of Juan!' Maria said, handing the picture over.

'Now we must go and get the elf-stone,' said the woman. 'In order for the spell to work, we must take the route through the cemetery.'

Maria was afraid. She didn't like cemeteries, and especially not in the evening when it was dark.

'Can't we go on the road around the cemetery instead?'

'For the spell to work, you must follow my instructions,' said the woman sternly. 'Do you want to marry Juan or not?'

'I do!' said Maria. 'I want to marry Juan very much. But I am afraid.'

'Don't be afraid,' said the woman. 'I have a cutlass in my belt to protect us from anything that would do us any harm.'

So Maria and the woman walked along the path through the cemetery. It was long and winding, and Maria was sure she could see strange shapes moving in the darkness.

At times she thought that she and the old woman were being followed but, every time she turned back to see, the wise old woman told her, 'Keep your eyes to the front. Don't look back!' And so Maria would turn back round and look only in front of her.

When they finally arrived at the opening to the forest, Maria was already wondering if it was a good idea to continue. A churning in her belly made her think that maybe she should go home and forget all about her dream of marrying Juan.

'Having second thoughts?' the woman said knowingly. 'Don't worry, it will be worth it in the end, when you have Juan as your husband.'

So Maria took a deep breath and they continued into the forest together.

'Come on, keep up!' the woman said, over and over.

Though the woman was old, she had a lot of energy and she marched with strong steps that Maria could hardly keep up with. The woman used her cutlass to cut through the bushes and overhanging trees and eventually they arrived at the small cave by the stream.

'Now let's look for an elf-stone,' said the woman. 'Remember, it will be in the shape of a man.'

Maria searched high and low amongst all the stones and pebbles by the side of the stream. They were all shapes and sizes but none looked to her like the shape of a man.

'There it is!' said the woman, pointing over to a pile of stones in the corner of the cave. To get to it they would have to walk along a thin ledge around a pool of greenish water and risk falling in. Maria held on to the cave wall and took her time. She edged her way around the cave, careful not to miss her footing. When she reached the pile of stones she pushed away the other ones and pulled out the elf-stone. It was true: the tiny stone had the shape of a man. But how the old woman had seen it from such a distance baffled her. With equally delicate steps, Maria made her way back around the ledge.

'Now, quickly, we must walk to the main crossroads so I can do my spell!' said the woman.

By now, Maria was tired. She wasn't sure if she would have enough energy to walk all the way to the main crossroads.

'I'm tired,' she said. 'Can we rest first?'

'We only have a short time to do this,' the woman said. 'We have to reach the crossroads as dawn breaks or the spell will not work. When the sun shines and the rain falls and the rainbow forms, that is when I must do my spell, then I will bury the picture with the elf-stone.'

'Very well,' said Maria, as she could see that the woman was losing her patience. 'Lead the way.'

The woman once again led the way with strong steps and Maria hurried along behind her. But as they rushed through the forest a stone hit Maria on the back of her head and she collapsed.

'What was that?' she said groggily.

The woman turned and looked and then said, 'That's the elf king. If he catches us with his stone our lives won't be worth living! Come on, we have to get away quickly!'

'But I feel dizzy and weak!' said Maria, rubbing her head. 'I can't run!'

So the old woman picked Maria up with a strength far beyond that of an old woman and she ran quickly with Maria in her arms, her feet hardly touching the ground. When they reached the main crossroads dawn was breaking and raindrops began to spill out of the clouds. Then there came a bright ray of sunshine and before long a magnificent colourful rainbow.

'It's time,' said the woman, and then she put the picture of Juan under the elf-stone on a small mound of dirt by her feet and she began to chant:

> *Juan and Maria,*
> *Juan and Maria,*
> *This be the union of Juan and Maria.'*

Then the old woman buried the picture and the elf-stone in the earth and smiled at Maria.

'It is done. You can go home now,' she said.

'And now will I marry Juan?' Maria asked.

'Certainly!' said the old woman.

Maria jumped for joy.

Later that morning, when Maria went to work, the most amazing thing happened. As Maria arrived at the big house, Juan was waiting at the door.

'Can I speak with you a moment?' he said, smiling at Maria. Maria was so overwhelmed that she didn't know what to say.

He continued, 'Today I am filled with courage to ask for your hand in marriage. Will you marry me?'

Without hesitation Maria said, 'Yes! I would love to marry you.'

Maria and Juan were married two days later. The wedding was a lavish one with all the trimmings. Juan paid for everything. Maria wore a magnificent lace wedding dress and she looked stunning in all her finery. Afterwards Juan bought a beautiful mansion for them to live in.

'You will want for nothing ever again!' Juan said to Maria. 'Everything I own now belongs to you also.'

Maria was very happy. Not only was she married to the man of her dreams, she was also one of the richest women in the district.

When the old woman went to collect the washing on the Friday, from Juan's parents' house, Maria went to meet her.

'Thank you so much,' Maria said. 'You have made me the happiest woman in the world.'

'Now you must pay me,' said the old woman. 'I want a

bag of gold coins for my service. Meet me at the cemetery gate with it at three o'clock.'

'You were right,' said Maria. 'Now I am married to Juan, I am rich too, so I will get a bag of gold coins out of the mansion vault, to pay you this afternoon.'

So that afternoon Maria went to the vault in the basement of the big mansion where she and Juan lived. There were gold coins and jewels and all manner of valuables there. She took a bag of gold coins and brought it to the cemetery gate at three o'clock, as was agreed.

But the old woman became greedy. 'I will come again this time next week, for the rest of the money,' she said.

'Oh,' said Maria. 'I thought, once I had paid you what you asked, that we would be finished.'

'I'll decide when we're done!' said the old woman.

Maria and Juan had a very happy marriage, but for one thing. Every week the old woman would order Maria to give her another bag of gold coins, but each time Maria gave the old woman the money, the old woman was never satisfied. The more money Maria gave her, the more money the old woman wanted, and every week she demanded more and more.

The old woman said if Maria didn't continue the payments then she would reverse the spell and the marriage with Juan would be over.

Now Maria felt terrible that she was taking bags of gold coins out of the vault without telling Juan, so one day she went to her husband and told him everything.

'Juan, my dear husband,' she said, 'I have done something I am ashamed of, but in my heart I did it because I loved you so much and didn't know what else to do. I am so afraid that when I tell you this I will lose you, but I do not want to keep anything from you any more. If I must lose you then lose you I must, but I want you to know the truth.'

Juan listened tentatively. 'Speak, my dear wife. Nothing you have to say will offend me. I love you. You will never lose me.'

So Maria told him everything, about how she had made a deal with the old woman, how she had stolen his photograph, how she had gone through the forest with the old woman to get the elf-stone, and how the woman had cast the spell to make him marry her.

Juan listened to what she had to say and then he was silent as he thought.

Eventually he spoke. 'I have loved you ever since I set eyes on you, from the first day you started working at my family's house. I loved the way you never fussed around me and I always wanted to get to know you. I was just too shy to speak to you. I didn't have the courage to talk to you. I spoke to you that morning because I thought I was going to lose you.'

'Lose me?' Maria asked, puzzled. 'Why would you think that?'

'The evening before I spoke to you, I saw you meet someone at the cemetery gates, and then you went into the forest with them. It was dark so I couldn't see who it was, but the man had a cutlass and you were chasing after him with a spring in your step. I thought he must be your love!'

Maria started to laugh. 'That wasn't a man, that was . . .'

Juan interrupted her. 'I know now from what you say that it was the old woman, but I was so jealous I could not tell. I was enraged and went to bed that night telling myself that I must let you know my true feelings in the morning. It was then that I asked you to marry me.'

'I see!' said Maria.

'So, my darling,' Juan said, 'the old woman didn't cast a spell at all. She has tricked you. It's all nonsense. I loved you all along and always wanted you to be my wife. You owe her nothing and you must stop payments to her immediately.'

Maria was a little nervous about stopping the payments to the old woman, afraid of what she might do. So Juan decided he would talk to the old woman himself and put an end to this nonsense.

Since the old woman had been getting the gold coins from Maria, she had stopped washing clothes for his family, and so she no longer came to the family house.

Juan went to meet her at the cemetery gate, where she was waiting for Maria to arrive with her gold coins.

'What are you doing here?' the old woman shrieked with horror.

'I know all about the rubbish you have been telling my wife!' Juan said. 'And I know about all the money you have been taking from her. You will not be getting any more money, so leave her alone!'

The old woman was angry and chased him all the way back to the mansion, shouting after him, 'It was a fair bargain! I want my money! I want my money! Thief! You'll regret breaking the deal!' But Juan didn't pay her any mind, he just ignored her cries.

But when he arrived and called for Maria, she was not there.

'Maria! Maria! Where are you?'

But she was nowhere to be found. The old woman laughed. 'It serves you right for not paying your debts!'

'What have you done to my wife?' Juan demanded.

'I have done nothing to her,' said the old woman, 'but if you were to give me more gold coins, I can help you find her.'

Desperate to find his wife, Juan agreed to pay the woman and reluctantly he took two more bags of gold coins from his vault and gave them to her.

'Lovely, lovely . . .' she said. 'Follow me!'

They searched all over the village, asking everyone they

saw if they had seen Maria, but to no avail. Finally the old woman suggested they go to the cave in the middle of the forest to see if the elf king knew of her whereabouts. Juan thought the old woman was still talking nonsense as he did not believe in the elf king one bit, but he needed to find his wife so he agreed to go along.

Juan rode on horseback while the woman marched with strong steps all the way to the small cave by the stream, never once stopping to rest. When they got to the cave, Juan dismounted and went inside. He could not believe what he saw in the greenish pool of water. There was Maria, with water up to her waist! Beside her, coming out of the water, was a tiny man with a long green beard. He was wearing a crown. Juan jumped into the water immediately but, as he reached to grab her, she disappeared. The little man disappeared too.

'That was Maria!' said Juan to the woman. 'Stop your hocus pocus and give her back to me!'

The old woman laughed. 'I want everything you own in return!'

'You can have it all!' said Juan. 'My wealth means nothing to me! I just want my wife back!'

The old woman made Juan sign a paper saying that everything he and Maria owned now belonged to her. Once he had done this she turned to the pool of water and said, 'Release!'

It was then the water in the greenish pool began to

whirl round and round. Maria and the elf king were pushed up to the surface. The elf king helped Maria to the edge of the pool.

'Now keep away from my cave!' he commanded as he disappeared into the water.

'Let's get out of here!' Juan said, clasping Maria's hand and leading her out to his horse.

Juan and Maria rode out of the forest as fast as they could. They rode to a far-off place where they went on to live a happy and simple life with no care for the wealth they had lost. They had each other and that was everything they had ever wanted.

As for the old woman, she was very rich and she lived the rest of her days in Juan and Maria's mansion. However, she was never satisfied: nothing was ever enough and she always wanted more.

Papa Bwa and Monkey Trouble

This story is based on a folk tale from Trinidad

Annie was a baker. She loved to bake cakes. All kinds – coconut cakes, lemon cakes, ginger cakes, chocolate cakes, banana cakes – any cakes you care to name, Annie made them all.

People loved Annie's cakes. They would come from far and wide to buy them at the market. Annie had a special stall there, with a sign above it which said ANNIE'S DELICIOUS CAKES. And delicious they were!

With the money Annie made from her cakes, she would buy the most amazing dresses. She liked to dress well, especially when she went dancing – which she loved to do.

Now, every morning, Annie would get up bright and early so that she could bake before she went to the market, which was a fair way from where she lived.

But on this particular morning, Annie didn't get up bright and early. She had been dancing the night before and had gone to bed long after midnight. She was very tired and had slept long past her usual time. When Annie finally awoke, she couldn't believe what time it was. She had so much to do – so many cakes to bake and so little time to bake them in!

Annie jumped out of bed and started baking as quickly as she could. When she had finally loaded the last of her cakes into her basket, she set off.

The market was in town and most people walking alone would walk the road around the forest to get there. So would Annie on her usual daily trip. However, on this day, Annie knew that if she were to take the long road around the forest she would never get to the market on time. Annie decided she would take the short cut through the forest itself to get to town.

Well, everyone knew that anyone walking alone through the forest should take great caution. It was known that Papa Bwa, the protector of the forest and everything in it, did not like too many people wandering around and disturbing his peace. Annie knew this, but she hoped that taking the short cut would not disturb Papa Bwa. After all, her plan was to dash through as quickly as possible.

She hoped very much that Papa Bwa wouldn't even notice she was there.

And in any case, Annie told herself, if by chance she were to disturb Papa Bwa's peace, she would let him know immediately that she was not a hunter. You see, Annie knew that Papa Bwa hated hunters and woodcutters and anyone or anything that threatened to hurt the forest and the creatures in it. Annie was sure that once she told Papa Bwa that she was not a hunter he would let her go on her way.

So Annie made her way through the dense forest. It was very dark. Annie had never been in the forest alone before, and the big trees and all the strange sounds and hoots coming from the forest creatures frightened her. She could hear them all, even at the forest entrance. Still, she was determined to get to the market on time, so she bravely marched through as quickly as she could.

As she walked Annie could hear the snapping of twigs and branches. At first she thought that it was coming from her own feet but, strangely, when she stopped walking she could still hear it. In fact, it was coming towards her! Afraid, Annie crouched behind a large tree.

As she peered out from her hiding place, Annie could see two hooves walking the forest floor. The creature's legs were hairy, as was its whole body, chest, shoulders and arms. But the head was that of an old man with two small horns. He had long white hair and a beard of leaves. He was tall like a giant and his arms and legs were muscular. Though Annie had never seen him before, she knew straight away that it was Papa Bwa.

'*Papa Bwa* . . .' Annie said to herself, her heart pounding. Although she didn't move an inch, she could see the creature sniffing the air and coming towards her. He could smell her cakes! What was she to do?

Remembering her plan, Annie stood up boldly and shouted, 'I am not a hunter!'

But Papa Bwa didn't appear to listen. He just kept on advancing towards her, looking so fierce and angry that Annie turned and ran away as quickly as her legs could carry her. The branches scratched her arms and cut her skin but still she ran. But Papa Bwa was not slowing down!

Annie ran and ran. She was afraid of what Papa Bwa might do to her if he caught her.

'I am not a hunter! I'm not a hunter!' she screamed as she ran.

A monkey was walking by (as this was a time before monkeys swung through trees) and, hearing all the commotion, looked to see what was going on. He saw Annie running for her life.

'Trouble is with me!' Annie shouted.

Monkey was curious as to what this 'trouble' was that the girl had, for he could see that Papa Bwa wanted it very badly.

'Trouble is with me!' Annie shouted again and again.

She threw the basket of cakes to the ground so she could run faster.

Still Papa Bwa carried on after her, never letting up. Annie ran and ran, with Papa Bwa hot on her tail. Eventually she saw the opening which led to the town, and she ran out of the forest to safety.

When Annie got to the market she had no cakes to sell. To everyone who came to buy from her she told the story of how she had foolishly walked through the forest alone and how Papa Bwa had chased her out. Annie vowed she would never walk through the forest alone again.

Meanwhile, Monkey was busy looking at the basket that the girl had left behind. It smelt good. He didn't know what the word *trouble* meant and he thought that when the girl was shouting, 'Trouble is with me!' she must have been talking about what she was carrying in the basket. He couldn't wait to see what was inside!

Monkey looked inside and found Annie's cakes. First he tried the coconut cakes. They tasted delicious and he ate them all up. 'Trouble is delicious!' he said to himself. Then he tried the lemon cakes. They tasted amazing and he ate them all up. 'Trouble is amazing!' he exclaimed. Then he tried the ginger cakes. They tasted very good and he ate them all up. 'Trouble is very good!' he cried out. Then he tried the chocolate cakes. They tasted superb and he ate them all up. 'Trouble is superb!' he declared. Then he got to the banana cakes and he had never tasted anything so incredibly delightful. 'Trouble is delightful!' he proclaimed. When Monkey had eaten the last of the cakes and he realized that there were none left he said, 'Hmmmmmmm, trouble tastes good. I want more trouble!'

Now, Monkey didn't know where to get more trouble from, so he decided to explore the direction from which Annie had come. He walked quickly through the forest and made his way to the very same opening in the forest that Annie had come through. Arriving on the road, Monkey saw a small shop. He went inside.

'I am looking for trouble!' he said to the shopkeeper.

Now, the shopkeeper thought that was a strange thing to ask for. No one had ever come to his shop looking for trouble before. He had known Monkey a long time and he didn't like Monkey much; he thought he was a bit foolish. The shopkeeper decided to have some fun with Monkey and trick him.

'You're looking for trouble, you say? I have plenty of it in my backyard. I will put it in a bag for you! How much do you want?'

'A lot,' said Monkey greedily. 'Give me all you have!'

'It will cost you plenty of money,' said the mischievous shopkeeper.

'No problem,' said Monkey. 'Trouble tastes so good, it is worth every penny.'

'Wait here,' said the shopkeeper and he went out through the back door.

Sleeping in the shopkeeper's backyard was the most ferocious wild dog you ever did see. The shopkeeper, careful not to wake it, put the dog in a big sack. He dragged the sack to the front of the shop and handed it to Monkey.

'Here you are,' the shopkeeper said, 'there's plenty of trouble for you inside that bag! The bag is heavy; be sure to drag it carefully so that the trouble doesn't get damaged.'

The greedy Monkey couldn't believe his luck. 'That sure is a big bag of trouble,' he said happily. He paid the shopkeeper all the money he had and carefully dragged the heavy bag out of the shop. He couldn't wait to get back to the forest and enjoy his feast of trouble.

Monkey dragged the bag on to the road and back the way he had come until he reached the forest. As he dragged the bag on the bumpy forest ground he heard a howl. Thinking it must have come from one of the forest creatures and reluctant to share his bag of trouble with anyone, he moved more quickly through the forest. The more he dragged the bag over the bumpy forest ground, the more the wild dog howled. And the more howls Monkey heard, the faster he moved through the forest. And so it continued until the wild dog inside the bag was howling so loudly that Papa Bwa himself came out to see what all the commotion was about.

*

Now Papa Bwa, the protector of the forest and all that lived there, was very concerned indeed. 'Which of my forest creatures is howling in pain?' he shouted, running towards Monkey. Before Monkey could answer, Papa Bwa ripped open the bag and set free the howling wild dog. The dog gnashed its teeth and growled, and Monkey was sure he was going to be eaten up! Where were those delicious cakes he had expected to find?

The wild dog jumped towards Monkey. Monkey ran up a tree. 'I was looking for trouble! I didn't know the wild dog was in the bag!'

Luckily, the wild dog could not climb the tree and so it stayed below, barking up at Monkey fiercely.

'Well, if you look for trouble you will find it!' Papa Bwa said triumphantly.

From that day to this, Monkey lives in trees, high up and away from the gnashing teeth of the wild dog! And all thanks to Annie and her delicious cakes.

The Singing Pepper Bush

This story is based on a folk tale from St Vincent

There were once a king and queen who loved each other very much. They lived in a beautiful palace and they were very, very rich. The king and queen had a son and a daughter, Prince Wilmot and Princess Louisa.

The queen was a lovely woman, always laughing and singing. She made everyone around her smile and no one had a bad word to say about her. Every day the queen would cook her husband the most delicious dishes, callaloo soup and roast breadfruit and saltfish and curried goat. She would always season the king's food with his favourite spice, the pepper grown on the pepper bush at the bottom of the palace gardens. If she had so wished, the queen could have employed a royal chef to cook all the meals, but this was not her wish. She took pleasure in watching her family enjoy the food she made.

One day the queen became very sick. Despite trying their very hardest, the doctors could not find a way to cure her.

Sadly, the queen died. The king was distraught, as were his children. The king was so sad that he lost his appetite and wouldn't eat. He stayed in bed every day. The newly appointed royal chef tried all sorts of recipes, but the king would not eat. He missed his wife dearly. The poor king got sadder and sadder, and very thin and weak.

Princess Louisa wanted to make her father smile again so, having watched her mother prepare her father's meals daily, she decided that she would pick some peppers from the pepper bush and cook him something. She took her time in the palace kitchen and seasoned the food just as she had seen her mother do. She brought the food to her father's bedroom on a tray.

When the king smelt the food that his daughter had brought to him, he sat up in his bed immediately. Tears welled in his eyes. The meal set before him smelt and looked as if it had been cooked by his wife and he couldn't wait to taste it. And he wasn't disappointed. The meal was delicious and tasted exactly like the food his wife used to cook.

'It is as if you have brought your mother back to me,' he

said gratefully to his daughter. Princess Louisa was pleased with herself for having made her father smile again, and every day after that she cooked her father something special, seasoned with the pepper picked from the pepper bush. Soon the king was out of bed and putting on weight and feeling well again. Though he still missed his wife, the king was able to enjoy spending time with his children.

One day an evil witch by the name of Melissa heard about the rich king who had lost his wife, and she tried to think of a way for her to get her hands on all his wealth. She decided she would trick the king into marrying her so that she could be queen and have all his riches.

The evil witch had powers that could make her look beautiful, so she transformed her set frown into an attractive smile and her cold, calculating eyes into warm, caring eyes, and made her way to the palace gates.

When the king saw Melissa, her smile reminded him of his wife as did her eyes, and he could not take his gaze off her. Caught under her spell, he asked her to marry him straight away. It was announced that the royal wedding would take place and everyone was glad that at last the king had found happiness once more.

All except Princess Louisa.

Princess Louisa was worried for her father. Who was this strange woman that he had immediately fallen in love with and why did they need to get married so soon after meeting?

'How can this be?' she said to her brother, Wilmot. 'Father can't be serious about getting married to this woman, can he?' But Prince Wilmot was happy for his father. He was glad that the king had been able to find happiness again.

'Father is happy,' he said, 'and we should be happy for him.'

And that was that. The wedding plans were set to go ahead.

But try as she might, Princess Louisa could not be happy for her father. She watched how Melissa, his bride-to-be, fussed over her father in public, but noticed that when she thought no one was looking her smile would turn into a scowl. Princess Louisa didn't know how to tell her father what she saw. She didn't want to spoil his happiness but she didn't trust Melissa at all.

Soon the day of the wedding arrived. Princess Louisa could take no more and she asked her father if he was sure about the marriage.

'I have not felt this happy for a long time!' said the king. 'I want to marry Melissa, my dear daughter. Please give me your blessing.'

So Princess Louisa had no choice. She gave her father her blessing and pretended that she was happy. She celebrated the wedding with her brother and all of the other guests for the sake of her father.

After the wedding, Princess Louisa continued to cook special dishes for her father, seasoned with the peppers from the pepper bush. The king loved her meals and praised his daughter for her fine recipes. Each time he ate he would delight in talking about his dead wife and how Princess Louisa's food made him feel like she had never left.

This did not please Queen Melissa. In fact, Queen Melissa was very jealous of the way the king spoke about Princess Louisa's mother and she disliked the way the king and his daughter laughed and joked as they remembered the dead queen fondly.

'From now on, *I* will cook your meals!' said Queen Melissa to the king.

'No!' said Princess Louisa. 'I know what my father likes! I will cook for him.'

The king agreed with his daughter. Louisa would continue to cook for him.

This made Queen Melissa very angry. She decided she would think up a plan to get rid of Princess Louisa. She would wait until the king was out of the palace and then she would put her plan into action.

One day the king and Prince Wilmot had to go into town on urgent business. They would be gone all day and all night, leaving Queen Melissa and Princess Louisa alone in the palace. Queen Melissa couldn't wait for the king and Prince Wilmot to leave. 'Off you go,' she said, waving them off. 'Hurry, hurry, make haste!'

It was the first time Princess Louisa was to be alone with the new queen and she wasn't looking forward to it. As soon as her father and brother left, Princess Louisa dashed up to her room.

Queen Melissa called her. 'Louisa, I have a job for you!' she said. 'I want you to sweep the yard.'

Princess Louisa wasn't accustomed to sweeping the yard and she was about to protest. There were palace staff that did that sort of thing so there was no need for the princess to do it. She knew that her stepmother was being spiteful, but she thought about how happy her father had been lately with his new wife and decided she would be an obedient stepdaughter for her father's sake.

'Very well,' Princess Louisa said politely, and she took a broom and began to sweep the yard.

Then Queen Melissa took a bunch of ripe bananas and hung them up in a tree.

'And one more thing,' said Queen Melissa as Princess Louisa swept the yard. 'I am going for a walk. While I am away, I want you to guard these fig bananas and make sure no birds peck at them.'

Now the evil Melissa knew very well that birds love to eat ripe bananas when they are hanging out in the open air like that and she knew Princess Louisa would have a hard job stopping any birds from pecking at them.

'If you let any birds peck at these fig bananas,' she said threateningly, 'I will bury you alive!' Princess Louisa could tell by the evil look in her stepmother's eye that she meant every word and she was afraid. Queen Melissa held her head up high and walked away.

'I will be coming back to check on the bananas in a little while so you had better make sure they haven't been pecked at!' she said. 'And this yard had better be clean too!'

Princess Louisa didn't know what to do. How was she supposed to stop birds from pecking at the bananas hanging on the tree? She began to sweep the yard as she had been told to do and hoped that no birds would fly down to peck at the ripe fig bananas.

Alas, before long a blackbird swooped down towards the bunch of ripe fig bananas hanging on the tree. At once Princess Louisa sang out:

> 'No, Blackbird, no,
> Don't take the fig!
> No, Blackbird, no,
> Don't take the fig!
> No, Blackbird, no,
> Don't take the fig!
> If you do, my stepmother will bury me alive.'

The blackbird heard Princess Louisa's song and took pity on her. It flew away and left the ripe fig bananas alone. No sooner had the blackbird left then a pigeon swooped down towards the bunch of ripe fig bananas hanging on the tree. At once Princess Louisa sang out:

'No, Pigeon, no,
Don't take the fig!
No, Pigeon, no,
Don't take the fig!
No, Pigeon, no,
Don't take the fig!
If you do, my stepmother will bury me alive.'

The pigeon heard Princess Louisa's song and took pity on her. It flew away and left the ripe fig bananas alone.

Princess Louisa was grateful that the birds had taken pity on her. She continued to sweep the yard until it was clean and as the sun went down she waited for her stepmother's return.

Then suddenly an owl swooped down towards the bunch of ripe fig bananas hanging on the tree. At once Princess Louisa sang out:

'No, Owl, no,
Don't take the fig!

No, Owl, no,
Don't take the fig!
No, Owl, no,
Don't take the fig!
If you do, my stepmother will bury me alive.'

But, alas, the owl did not take pity on Princess Louisa. Instead the owl pecked at the ripe fig bananas, just as the wicked stepmother was returning from her walk.

'Did I not tell you to guard the fig bananas?' said Queen Melissa.

'And I tried to stop them, but the owl would not listen to me!' pleaded Princess Louisa.

'Oh dear,' said Queen Melissa menacingly. 'Now I must bury you alive, as I said I would!' And the evil witch grabbed Princess Louisa and dragged her to the bottom of the palace garden. She dug a hole beside the pepper bush where Princess Louisa had picked the peppers for her father's meals and threw Princess Louisa in the hole. She buried her alive.

The next day, when the king and Prince Wilmot came home, the king asked for his daughter. Queen Melissa denied any knowledge of where Princess Louisa was. 'I haven't seen her since yesterday. I thought she followed you into town!' said Queen Melissa.

The king was very worried and sent out a royal search

party to find his daughter but it seemed she was nowhere to be found. The king was very sad, as was Prince Wilmot. The king was so sad that, once again, he lost his appetite and wouldn't eat. He stayed in bed every day. He missed his daughter dreadfully. The poor king got sadder and sadder, and very thin and weak.

'I know what will make you feel better,' said the prince. 'I will make you a meal seasoned with your favourite spice – pepper from the pepper bush.'

'I'll do it!' said Queen Melissa, but the king stopped her.

'Let Wilmot do it. He used to watch my beloved wife and my sweet daughter prepare my food so he knows how I like it.'

So Prince Wilmot went to pick some peppers from the pepper bush to make his father a special meal. But when Prince Wilmot went to pick the peppers, the pepper bush began to sing:

> 'No, Brother, no,
> Don't stamp on me!
> No, Brother, no,
> Don't stamp on me!
> No, Brother, no,
> Don't stamp on me!
> For my stepmother has buried me alive.'

Prince Wilmot couldn't believe what he was hearing. He ran to his sick father's room at once and told him what he had heard.

'Nonsense!' said the king. 'Pepper bushes don't sing!' And he sent his son to have a lie down, believing him to be sick.

'Now *I* will go and pick the peppers,' said Queen Melissa, and off she went.

But when Queen Melissa reached the pepper bush and stretched out her hand to pick a pepper, the pepper bush pulled away from her. She couldn't get her fingers on a single pepper to pick. She tried over and over again but, each time she tried, the same thing happened and she could not pick a pepper. She went back to the king empty-handed.

'Where are the peppers?' asked the king.

'I couldn't pick any!' said Queen Melissa. 'Every time I tried to take one, I couldn't get my fingers on it.'

The king thought Queen Melissa had gone mad and decided to get out of bed and pick the peppers himself. By now he was very weak as he hadn't eaten for days, and Prince Wilmot got out of bed and decided to go with him. Queen Melissa followed them too. When the king arrived at the pepper bush, he picked some peppers straight away.

But then, just as before, the bush started to sing in Princess Louisa's voice:

'No, Father, no,
Don't stamp on me!
No, Father, no,
Don't stamp on me!
No, Father, no,
Don't stamp on me!
For my stepmother has buried me alive.'

At once Queen Melissa felt nervous. Prince Wilmot, who had heard the singing once before, fetched a shovel and quickly began to dig up the dirt by the pepper bush. There she was, Princess Louisa, alive and well!

'Father, Melissa buried me alive!' Princess Louisa cried.

And the wicked witch, Melissa, ran as fast as she could away from the palace and was never seen again.

Compère Lapin and the Good Sense

*This story is based on a folk tale from
St Lucia and the Commonwealth of Dominica*

Now, good sense is something most people don't have enough of. Good sense tells you to carry an umbrella with you when the clouds look grey, or tells you to look left and right to be safe when you're crossing a road, or to eat all your greens in order to stay healthy. It has been said that there was a time when good sense grew on trees. They say you could even find it in a flower or a bush, or stuffed in a corner or behind a wall or just sitting there on the ground. Well, so I have heard.

The trouble with good sense was that it wasn't easily visible. It did have a blue hue, which you could see shimmering if you squinted but, because it was so difficult to spot, some folks could not get their hands on it easily.

The animals in the forest would compete on a special day every year called Good Sense Day to see who could find and collect the most good sense, and the winner would get a trophy for his or her efforts.

Now Compère Lapin was a troublesome rabbit, always trying to get more than his fair share of anything he could get his hands on. When Good Sense Day arrived that year, Compère Lapin woke up with a fine plan. Not only did he want to collect the *most* good sense, Compère Lapin wanted to have *all* of the good sense for himself! The thing was, Compère Lapin didn't want to collect the good sense himself. He wanted to relax while everyone else collected the good sense for him.

So on the day of the annual competition Compère Lapin watched as all the animals scurried around the forest trying to collect as much good sense as they could. While they all scurried around, he did nothing but relax in the sun. The rest of the animals were not impressed.

'That rascal Compère Lapin thinks he can get away with doing nothing whilst we do all the work!' said Compère Dog.

'Well, he'd better not think he's getting any of my good sense!' clucked Compère Cockerel.

'Or mine,' said Compère Goat.

When all the animals had collected as much good sense

as they could carry, Compère Owl did his best to count up to see who had the biggest pile. It was announced that Compère Duck was this year's winner and, as Compère Owl presented him with the Good Sense trophy, Compère Lapin took the opportunity to step forward and say, 'Wait! Wait! There's a problem!'

No one was really surprised to see Compère Lapin step forward, as they knew he was up to something. They were curious, though, to hear what he had to say.

'The problem,' said Compère Lapin, 'is storage. Every year we collect all this good sense and we have piles and piles of it, but nowhere to put it! When all that good sense is left hanging around, it could cause all sorts of accidents.'

The other animals could not recall any accidents being caused by the lack of storage for good sense. But no one wanted to be thought uncaring, so they all agreed that finding some storage for the good sense was a great idea.

'Well,' said Compère Lapin, 'I suggest we put it all in one place and have someone look after it.'

'Good idea!' said Compère Turtle. Compère Frog and all the other animals agreed.

'Just give me all your piles of good sense,' said Compère Lapin, 'and I'll look after it all for you.'

Well, the animals weren't sure about that! Compère Lapin wasn't very trustworthy and they were reluctant to hand over all the good sense they had collected just like that.

'How do we know you won't steal it from us?' Compère Frog croaked.

Compère Lapin was taken aback. 'I'm not a thief,' he said angrily. 'But just to prove that I have no interest in your good sense, I will give everyone a receipt.'

The animals talked amongst themselves and agreed that getting a receipt from Compère Lapin was a good idea. At least they would know which good sense belonged to whom. So all the animals gave the good sense that they had collected to Compère Lapin, and Compère Lapin gave each of them a receipt. It seemed like a perfect plan and everyone was happy – but especially Compère Lapin, who had no intention of giving any of the animals back their good sense, receipt or no receipt!

Once Compère Lapin had everyone's good sense and all the animals had gone home, he poured it all into a big iron cooking pot. He decided he would hang the pot at the top of a big tree in the centre of the forest, far out of the reach of the other animals. He laughed at how foolish they had been, handing over their good sense for him to take care of. Well, he was going to take care of it all right! Now all the good sense belonged to him!

Compère Lapin dragged the big iron cooking pot to the tree at the centre of the forest. But as he tried to climb the tree, pot in hand, he found the pot was far too big.

Compère Lapin didn't listen to the good sense telling him that it wasn't a good idea to be climbing so high with a big pot, and it wasn't long before he lost his balance and dropped the pot. All of the good sense that had been collected scattered all around the forest.

Compère Lapin was vexed. He hopped around angrily, moaning about how he had lost all the good sense he had tricked the others into handing over.

When the animals in the forest each came to Compère Lapin bringing their receipts and asking for their portion of good sense, Compère Lapin told them he had tried to keep hold of the good sense for them but, despite his efforts, it had decided to flee from him, so they would have to wait until next Good Sense Day to get some more. The animals were not happy and vowed they would never let Compère Lapin trick them again!

Compère Lapin Looks for Wisdom

This story is based on a folk tale from
St Lucia and the Commonwealth of Dominica

One day Compère Lapin went to see God and said, 'You're the wisest of them all! If only I could be wise like you!'

'No one can be wise like me,' said God.

'That's just not fair!' said Compère Lapin. 'Keeping all that wisdom for yourself is just GREEDY!'

Well, God thought about what Compère Lapin said. God liked to be fair and he certainly wasn't greedy.

'Very well,' God said. 'If you can pass some tests then I will give you some wisdom!'

Compère Lapin was intrigued, 'What are these tests?' he asked.

'There are three impossible tasks,' said God. 'If you can do these three tasks, I will give you some wisdom. First, bring me the scales of the greatest, biggest sea fish. Second, bring me milk from a wild cow. Third, bring me two teeth from the mouth of a living crocodile.'

Now, Compère Lapin wasn't one to be beaten and, although the tasks that God had set him seemed to be impossible, he was ready to take on the challenge.

'Very well,' said Compère Lapin. 'I will bring you the scales of the greatest, biggest sea fish, and I will bring you milk from a wild cow, and I will bring you two teeth from the mouth of a living crocodile.'

Compère Lapin had no idea how he was going to get those things and bring them to God. He went home to think up a plan.

Compère Lapin liked to play his drum when he had a problem. Tapping a rhythm on his drum always helped him to relax. His children liked to listen to him play too, as they liked to dance. So as Compère Lapin played his drum, his children danced.

Suddenly an idea came to him. Compère Lapin ran out of his house, still carrying his drum, and ran all the way to the edge of the sea. Once there, he began to play his drum, making rhythms that called all the fish in the sea to come up and dance. At first little fish appeared, popping their heads out of the water one by one. They came out of the water and danced all around Compère Lapin, but he was far from satisfied.

'This music is for the great big sea fish,' said Compère Lapin. 'Surely there are bigger fish than you in the sea?'

'Play louder!' said the little fish. 'The bigger fish are lower down in the sea so they cannot hear you!'

So Compère Lapin played his drum even louder and more rhythmically than before. Larger fish popped their heads out of the water and then they too came out of the water and danced all around him. But still Compère Lapin wasn't satisfied.

'This music is for the great big sea fish,' said Compère Lapin. 'Surely there are bigger fish than you in the sea? Where is the greatest, biggest fish of all?'

'Play louder!' said the larger fish. 'The great big fish is lower down in the sea so he cannot hear you!'

So Compère Lapin played his drum even louder and more rhythmically than before. At last, the greatest, biggest fish of all popped his head out of the water. Compère Lapin was overwhelmed by its great size. The greatest, biggest fish of all did not dance and he would not come out of the water. He simply watched.

Compère Lapin called out to the greatest, biggest fish of all: 'Great One, come and play the drum while I dance!' And the greatest, biggest fish of all came out of the water and played Compère Lapin's drum while he danced. After a while Compère Lapin stopped dancing and said, 'Now I will play the drum while you dance!'

And so Compère Lapin played the drum while the greatest, biggest fish of them all danced. Then Compère Lapin said, 'I am tired. I will lie down and take a rest while you watch over me,' and Compère Lapin lay down and rested and the greatest, biggest fish of all watched over him. After a while Compère Lapin said, 'Now you rest and lie down and I will watch over you.' And the greatest, biggest fish of all lay down.

As soon as he did so, Compère Lapin knocked unconscious the greatest, biggest fish of them all, and removed his scales. Compère Lapin took the scales and presented them to God.

'Fine,' said God. 'You have two more tasks. Now go into the woods and bring me milk from a wild cow.'

Compère Lapin had no idea how he was going to get milk from a wild cow.

But he went home and picked up a small gourd to carry the milk, and set off to the woods. He wandered around, trying to think of a way to get the milk until he stumbled on a large softwood tree and suddenly had an idea.

Compère Lapin climbed to the top of the tree and, once at the top, he began to call for a wild cow. 'Wild cow! Wild cow! Come and get me if you can, wild cow!'

Everyone in the forest knew that wild cows were not to be messed with.

'Who is calling me in such a disrespectful way?' called a wild cow.

'It's me, Compère Lapin, you weak, pathetic wild cow!'

The wild cow followed the sound of Compère Lapin's voice and charged into the centre of the forest. She looked for Compère Lapin but couldn't see him anywhere.

'Where are you? I can't see you!' she said.

'I'm up here in this tree!' said Compère Lapin.

'You had better come down here so I can mash you up!' said the wild cow.

'Mash me up?' laughed Compère Lapin. 'I've heard that you've lost all your strength and you couldn't even hurt a tiny little fly!'

'That's a lie!' said the wild cow. 'I am the strongest beast in the woods!'

'You are so weak!' laughed Compère Lapin from his great height in the tree. 'You couldn't even knock this tree down!'

'Oh yes I can!' said the wild cow.

'Let me see you do it then,' goaded Compère Lapin.

The wild cow couldn't wait to show Compère Lapin that she could knock down the tree. She put her head down and charged, horns first. But, because the bark of the tree was soft, her horns went deep into the trunk and stuck fast.

'I'm stuck!' she said. 'My horns are stuck in the tree!'

'Are you sure?' asked Compère Lapin.

'Yes, I'm certain,' said the wild cow, trying to move her head.

'Well, if you're sure then I'll come down,' said Compère Lapin.

When Compère Lapin got down from the top of the tree, he took the milk from the wild cow. When his small gourd was full of milk he presented it to God.

'Fine,' said God. 'You now have only one more task to complete. But this task is truly impossible. There is no way you can bring me two teeth from the mouth of a living crocodile!'

Compère Lapin had no idea how he was going to complete this third and final task, but he knew if he did then God would give him wisdom. He needed to find a way to get the two teeth from a living crocodile.

He went home to think and while he was bathing Compère Lapin had a brilliant idea. He asked his wife to bring him all the soap in the house and then when she had done this he marched over to a trail that he knew Compère Crocodile used on the hill that led to the river. Compère Lapin spread soap on the trail from Compère Crocodile's house at the top of the hill all the way to the bottom of the hill, and at the bottom of the hill he placed a large rock. Then he called out: 'Compère Crocodile! Compère

Crocodile! Come quickly! At the bottom of the trail there is a dead rabbit to eat!' And then he lay down near the rock and pretended to be dead.

Just as he had expected, Compère Crocodile came out of his house and saw Compère Lapin lying down at the bottom of the hill. He immediately started down the hill to eat Compère Lapin but as he did so he began to slip on the soap. He slipped faster and faster until he crashed into the large rock. When his big jaw hit the rock two teeth were knocked out and Compère Lapin jumped up and caught the teeth. He brought them to God and God was amazed.

'You brought me the scales from the greatest, biggest sea fish, milk from a wild cow, and two teeth from the mouth of a living crocodile!' said God.

'That's right,' said Compère Lapin. 'I brought you the three impossible things you asked for and you promised me wisdom in return.'

God pondered on what Compère Lapin had said.

'It required great wisdom for you to get these three impossible things,' said God. 'You already have wisdom!'

Compère Lapin thought about what God had said. It was true: while he had been looking for wisdom, he hadn't realized that he had used wisdom to complete the three impossible tasks and had what he was looking for all along!

The Spirit of the Rock

This story is based on a Carib legend from the Commonwealth of Dominica

Long, long ago there lived a Carib woman called Martha. Martha's husband, Joe, was a cruel, horrible man and he treated Martha badly.

Every morning when the cock crowed, Joe would shout at the top of his voice, 'Martha! Martha! Wake up and do your chores!'

Martha would wake up and shout back, 'Stop ordering me about! I am not your servant, I am your wife!'

And Joe would laugh and shake his head. 'That's right, you are my wife and I am your husband, so you must do as I say!'

Now Martha was no pushover by any means but she didn't like to fight, and she knew from past experience that her husband would only huff and puff and get himself in a right old state if she did not do as he said. So for the sake of peace and quiet, Martha would get up without a fuss every morning bright and early and get on with the chores. As she did so, Joe would jump into his hammock and go to sleep.

Martha's work started very early in the morning. First she would go fishing. Then she would come back to the house before Joe and her baby were awake and she would clean then cook the fish. After that, she would bathe and dress her baby and feed her family breakfast. At lunchtime she would give them their lunch, and in the afternoon she would strap her baby to her back and take the long walk to work the fields.

Along the way she could smell the sweet scent of flowers, and this was the best part of Martha's day. When she returned home, she would find her husband still relaxing in his hammock and as soon as he heard her return he would call, 'Martha! Martha! Don't you know you have work to do?' and she would hold her tongue to avoid a fight.

At night-time Martha's husband got out of his hammock and went to parties in the village. He danced and made merry all night long. In the early hours of the morning he would return home and as the cock crowed he would shout at the top of his voice, 'Martha! Martha! Wake up and do your chores!' Then he would climb into his hammock and sleep.

Every day was the same for the Carib woman Martha. While her husband relaxed, she did all the work!

Until one day . . .

While Martha was fishing, a funny thing happened. She was looking at her reflection in the water, shaking her head and saying, 'Why, oh why, do I live such a horrible life?' when she saw something strange.

Staring back at her from the water was the face of a wise old woman. Martha looked behind her but there was nobody there. When Martha looked back in the water, the wise woman's face began to sparkle and shimmer in the water and then she spoke with a gentle, reassuring voice.

'Lady, I know you are sad and tired, but things will get better.'

Martha gasped with amazement, but the wise old woman carried on speaking.

'Listen to me carefully,' she said. 'You see that rock over there?'

Martha looked in the distance and saw a huge rock up on the hillside.

'Yes, I see it,' she said.

'That's the Pegua Rock,' said the wise old woman. 'On top of that rock grow all manner of charms, but the one you need is the white flower with so sweet a scent that people passing on the highway at the foot of the cliff stop to savour it.'

'Oh yes,' said Martha, 'I have smelt that sweet scent many times on my long walk from working in the fields!'

'Well,' said the wise old woman, 'that flower is special. When it is in bloom, a new flower comes every hour of the day, and every hour another fades and falls.'

'What a peculiar flower, to only live for an hour,' said Martha.

'If you are lucky enough to get one of these flowers,' said the wise old woman, 'you may command whom you will with it.'

'Really?' said Martha, immediately thinking of her husband. With this flower, she could take command of her husband and stop him from being terrible to her.

'But if you go to the rock seeking this flower,' said the wise old woman, 'be sure to take with you some fine tobacco as a gift to the Spirit of the Rock.'

'The Spirit of the Rock?' gulped Martha.

'Why yes,' said the wise old woman, 'for the spirit guards the flower . . .'

'Very well,' said Martha, looking up at the rock. When she looked back again at the water she saw only her own reflection. The wise old woman had gone.

Martha continued to fish, thinking all the while. Could what she had just seen be true? Did a wise old woman really speak to her from out of the water? And was there such a thing as a magical flower that she could use to command her husband?

When Martha got home, as usual she cleaned and cooked the fish. Afterwards she bathed and dressed her baby and fed her family their breakfast.

At lunchtime she gave them their lunch and afterwards her mind started to ponder all the wise old woman had said. She longed for a time when her life could be her own again.

That afternoon, as usual, Martha strapped her baby to her back and took the long walk to work the fields. Along the way she could smell the sweet scent of flowers and she thought hard about how she might get to the rock without alerting suspicions from her husband.

As she worked the fields, she thought and thought about a better life and, on her walk back along the highway, the beautiful scent of the special white flower on the top of the Pegua Rock wafted down to her once more.

'If only I could get one of those flowers,' Martha said to herself. The rock seemed so far away.

When Martha arrived home, she found her husband still relaxing in his hammock. As soon as he heard her return, he called loudly, 'Martha! Martha! Don't you know you have work to do?' and she held her tongue.

That evening, as usual, Martha cooked supper and her husband got up from his hammock to eat the fish and cassava bread that she had prepared.

'What's wrong with you?' he said to Martha angrily. 'You have such a faraway look in your eye. I don't like it.' Before Martha could answer, Joe put on his hat and his coat and said, 'I'll see you in the morning.' Martha bid him goodnight with a nod of her head, and the door slammed shut behind him.

But although she was tired Martha just could not sleep. She tossed and turned in her bed. At last, she decided to sit outside and take in the night air. It was peaceful, sitting alone with her thoughts. From her home she could see the Pegua Rock in the moonlight, high up on the hillside.

If only she could get to one of those flowers, she thought. *If only . . .*

That night when her husband came home Martha was still outside. She hid as he went straight to his hammock and fell asleep. As she watched him sleep, she knew that she could no longer continue to live as her husband's slave. Knowing he would wake as soon as the cock crowed to give her his usual orders, Martha hurriedly searched his things for some tobacco to take with her as a gift for the Spirit of the Rock. She found a stash of tobacco by his pipe and wrapped some of it in paper to take with her. Then she left her fishing things close to her husband's hammock, grabbed some of the leftover cassava bread and a little water. She then took her beloved baby and set out on the long walk to the Pegua Rock.

When they reached the Pegua Rock, Martha sat her child down and gave her the bread to eat and a little of the water. Then she climbed a little until she reached a crack on the top of the rock. The crack went right the way through to the inside, and Martha guessed that it was where the spirit lived.

'Spirit of the Rock!' she called. 'Spirit of the Rock!'

And a low voice came from the crack in the rock. 'It is I. Who goes there?'

'I am Martha, the wife of a lazy man who does nothing all day while I do all the work. At night he goes out to parties and stays out all night! I have always been a good wife to this man.'

'And what do you want from me?' asked the spirit.

'I bring you an offering of tobacco,' said Martha, feeding the tobacco into the crack in the rock.

The Spirit of the Rock was pleased. He laughed happily. 'Take a flower,' he said. 'As soon as it blooms, take it and bathe in the river with it before it dies.'

Martha waited patiently for a fresh flower to bloom and then she picked it gently. The delicate white petals glowed in the sunlight and the sweet scent was intoxicating. She took her child, and hurriedly went down to the Pegua River to bathe. And when she had bathed she rubbed the flower all over her body and flung the shreds in the wind. They disappeared immediately.

Martha had no sooner left the river than she heard her husband coming after her with the fishing things she had left behind.

'Martha!' he called. 'Don't you know you have work to do?'

Martha bravely answered, 'I am no longer your slave! You have been a lazy, selfish husband and I have had enough!' And as she spoke there was a whoosh of a soft breeze and her husband was transformed into a bird with a bright yellow beak and claws.

'What can I do for you?' the bird said. 'I am here to serve you.'

'Then you can start by catching some fish to feed me and your child,' Martha said. The bird flew off immediately to fetch fish from the river. And from that day on Martha never had to do a day's work again for as long as she lived.

The Elephant Drum

This story is based on a folk tale from Haiti

There was once an old king with three sons. The youngest son of the three, Emmanuel, was known to be his favourite. The elder two brothers were very jealous of him.

One day the king became very sick and worried that he might die. He decided that he wanted to find out which of his sons loved him the most, so asked each of them how, once he had died, they would celebrate his life at his funeral.

The two eldest sons knew that if they could please their father with their answer he would reward them well, but the third son, Emmanuel, thought hard about his answer as he wanted to be honest.

The first son answered by saying, 'Father, because I love you so much, when the time comes for you to leave us, I will weep and weep and weep. We will have a quiet funeral as it would be a shame to waste all your wealth on anything too fancy. Your loss will be too great for me to bear, and after you are gone I will not allow anyone in this kingdom ever to smile again.'

'Son, I can see from your answer that you truly love me,' said the king.

When it came for the second son to answer, he said, 'Father, because I love you so much, when the time comes for you to leave us, I will weep and weep and weep. We will have a quiet funeral as it would be a shame to waste your wealth on anything too fancy. Your loss will be too great for me to bear, and after you are gone I will not allow anyone in this kingdom ever to speak again.'

'Son, I can see from the answer you have given that you and your brother love me equally,' said the king to his second son.

The king then turned to his third son and asked the same question.

Emmanuel answered thoughtfully. 'Father,' he said, 'truly I love you very much, but when you are gone I will not cry. Instead, I will remember all the good times we have shared and I will be happy.'

The father felt insulted. 'You will not cry when I am gone?' he asked.

'Father, we have had so many good times,' said Emmanuel, 'and for that I am grateful.'

The king thought about what his son had said. It was true. 'It is true, son. We have had many pleasurable times. But . . .'

Emmanuel interrupted him. 'I will not mourn you when you are gone. I will celebrate your life and spend plenty of your money on a big party!'

The king was taken aback at Emmanuel's words and the first two sons started to nudge each other and smile. They knew that the answer their younger brother had given was not what the king had expected to hear from his favourite son. They hoped that the king would disown Emmanuel and leave all his worldly goods to them when he died instead.

Emmanuel noticed that his father looked sad and in a bid to make him smile again he said, 'It will be the finest of celebrations. We will make fete and party and dance all night to the drum of the Elephant Queen.'

Now the king began to smile. The drum of the Elephant Queen was a special drum, sacred and hidden in a secret place.

'You would do that for me?' he asked. 'Son, I can see from the answer you have given me that you love me more than your brothers.'

The king was content with all of his sons' answers but he liked the answer that his favourite son had given him the most.

As the days went by the king became sicker and he called his son Emmanuel into his room.

'I fear I may not have many days left, my son. You must prepare for my funeral. Go and get the drum belonging to the Elephant Queen so you can celebrate my life, as you promised.'

Suddenly Emmanuel began to regret what he had said to his father. He had become carried away in trying to please his father, and had foolishly promised him something that would be impossible to get. He had no idea where to find the drum of the Elephant Queen.

It was said in those parts that, whenever it thundered, the sound of the rumbling was the sound of the elephants gathering together to dance and play drums in a sacred and special place. No one knew if this was true and, even if it was, no one knew where this sacred and special place might be. How could Emmanuel have been so foolish as to promise such an impossible thing to his dying father?

Despite not knowing where to start in his search, Emmanuel packed a parcel of food and set off to the village. He asked everyone he passed if they knew the way to the place where the elephants danced to the drum of the Elephant Queen, but nobody knew how to help him. Tired and frustrated, he stopped for a bite to eat.

As he ate, a blind beggar with a stick came towards him. 'That smells good,' the beggar said. 'Please could you give me a piece of whatever you are eating?'

Though he didn't have very much food to last him his journey, Emmanuel broke a piece of cornbread from his loaf and gave it to the blind beggar.

'Thank you, kind sir,' said the blind beggar.

'If you were not blind, I would ask if you have seen the place where the elephants dance to the drum of the Elephant Queen,' said Emmanuel.

The blind beggar laughed. 'Not even those who have eyes have seen such a place,' he said. The blind beggar enjoyed his cornbread and then he wished Emmanuel luck in his search and went on his way.

Emmanuel walked until dark, asking everyone he saw on the way if they knew where he might find the place where the elephants dance to the drum of the Elephant Queen. No one could help him. That night he slept in the grass at the edge of the road and in the morning he woke and carried on with his search. He walked and he walked, asking everyone he met along the way for directions. Nobody could help him. At midday, as the sun shone on his back, Emmanuel decided he would take a rest under the shade of a tree. He sat down and took out his parcel of food. As he did so a crippled man on crutches came to join him. The man had only one foot.

'Please could you give me a morsel of what you are eating?' said the crippled man. 'I am so hungry.'

Though Emmanuel only had a little food left and not much at all for the journey ahead of him, he broke a piece of cornbread from his loaf and gave it to the man. The man was a jolly fellow and had plenty of jokes to share with Emmanuel. But he too had no idea where to find the place where the elephants dance to the drum of the Elephant Queen.

'I am no better off than you are,' said Emmanuel. 'You may only have one leg and you may not be able to travel far, but though I can travel far with two legs I still don't know how to find the great drum of the Elephant Queen.' The crippled man thanked Emmanuel for the food and wished him well in his search before he left.

Emmanuel walked and walked, asking everyone he met along the way if they knew where he could find the great drum of the Elephant Queen. Nobody knew how to help him. Night-time fell and Emmanuel was feeling cold and hungry.

Sitting at the side of the road was an old man by a fire. He called over to Emmanuel, 'Come and join me. You look cold and tired.'

Emmanuel went and sat beside the man and opened up his parcel of food. 'Would you like some cornbread?' he asked the old man, though he knew the tiny morsel he had left was barely enough for one.

'Yes please,' said the man, and Emmanuel broke his small piece of cornbread in two and shared it with the man.

'Thank you,' the old man said. 'How very kind of you

to give me this third piece of cornbread. I also thank you for the second piece and the first piece.'

Emmanuel looked confused. 'I have only given you one piece!'

The man shook his head.

'I was the blind beggar man with whom you shared your cornbread, and I was also the crippled man you fed.'

Emmanuel was shocked.

'I am not a blind beggar or a crippled man or indeed an old man. I am a wizard with magical powers, and I can help you find the drum of the Elephant Queen.'

'You can?' said Emmanuel excitedly. 'Which way do I need to go?'

'First you must listen to what I have to say,' said the wizard. He stared into the fire and then spoke again. 'Go north across the grassland and after a while you will get to a giant mapou tree. You must climb it and wait there. It is here that the Queen of the Elephants plays her drum and the rest of the elephants come to dance. She will play her drum and they will dance until they are tired and then they will fall asleep. When they are asleep you will have your chance to take the Elephant Queen's drum. You'll have to be quick because if she catches you you'll be done for. I can give you four special stones to protect you. Use them wisely.'

The wizard gave Emmanuel four blue stones and as the fire went out he disappeared.

Emmanuel slept by the roadside and the following morning he woke up full of excitement, ready to find the Elephant Queen's drum.

He went north across the grassland as the wizard had instructed, until he reached the giant mapou tree. Then he climbed to the top and waited all day. There was no sign of any elephants.

As night began to fall Emmanuel could hear the sound of drumming in the distance. The drumming got louder and louder, and now Emmanuel could see a herd of elephants approaching, led by a queen.

He was so excited to see them but he was also very scared. Supposing they saw him, what would he do? He held on tight to the branches of the tree and kept very still as the elephants danced through the grassland and circled the giant mapou tree.

As the Elephant Queen played the drum, the rest of the elephants danced, linking their trunks, dipping and rising gracefully in a surprisingly delicate way. Their bodies moved to the beat as if their lives depended on its steady rhythm. The dance went on all night, but eventually the elephants became tired, stopped dancing and slept. When the last of the elephants was asleep the Queen stopped her drumming and went to sleep too.

Once he was sure they were all asleep, Emmanuel climbed down the tree. He found himself in the centre of a circle of sleeping elephants. He crept over to the sleeping

Elephant Queen and carefully eased the drum away from her. He put it on his head and climbed back over the sleeping elephants and out of the circle.

He started to run as fast as he could through the grassland to get away before they woke up.

But just when he thought he was safe, Emmanuel heard a rumbling sound. When he looked behind him he saw the Elephant Queen and all the angry elephants coming after him! Emmanuel ran and ran, but the elephants were catching up to him quickly.

Remembering the special blue stones that the wizard had given him, Emmanuel waited until the elephants were close and then he threw one of the stones behind him. Immediately a pine forest grew where the blue stone had fallen, obstructing the elephants' path. Emmanuel ran on a little further.

'Knock down the trees! Knock down the trees!' the Elephant Queen commanded, and all the elephants began to knock down the trees one by one. Before long, Emmanuel could hear the elephants coming after him once again.

He took another of the special blue stones and he threw it behind him. This time where the blue stone fell a large freshwater lake appeared, obstructing the elephants' path.

'Drink the water! Drink the water!' the Elephant Queen commanded, and all the elephants began to drink the water from the lake until it was low enough for the elephants to pass through.

Emmanuel had almost crossed the grassland when he noticed the elephants were still coming after him. He took the third blue stone and threw it behind him. This time a large saltwater lake appeared where the stone fell, obstructing the elephants' path.

'Drink the water! Drink the water!' the Elephant Queen commanded, and all the elephants began to drink the water from the saltwater lake.

But the salty water was making the elephants sick and they stopped drinking. The Elephant Queen didn't care and kept on shouting, 'Drink the water! Drink the water!'

The elephants carried on drinking the salty water until, one by one, each of the sick elephants collapsed on the ground and died. But the Elephant Queen, who didn't drink any of the water, was still coming after Emmanuel.

Emmanuel ran out of the grassland and made his way home. He went straight to his father's sickbed but his father wasn't there.

In the time that Emmanuel had been away, his father had become well again and he was busy working in the fields with Emmanuel's brothers. When he saw his favourite son had returned, Emmanuel's father was overjoyed. He hugged and kissed Emmanuel.

'I was foolish to send you off on that dangerous journey to find the elephant drum!' said Emmanuel's father. 'I could have lost you. Thank goodness you are home safely!'

That evening, Emmanuel, his father and his brothers

had a big celebration to mark Emmanuel's return. Emmanuel played the elephant drum and his father and brothers danced happily, glad to be all together again.

But as Emmanuel played the drum, they heard a heavy thumping on the ground. The angry Elephant Queen had heard the drumming and she had found her way to the village. She was heading straight to Emmanuel's father's home.

'Give me my drum! Give me my drum!' she cried. When she arrived at the house she grabbed the elephant drum from Emmanuel.

Afraid of what she might do to him, Emmanuel quickly took the last of the special blue stones that the wizard had given him and he threw it on the ground.

The large elephant drum broke into many pieces and each became a small drum. The Elephant Queen too broke into many pieces, and each piece of her became a drummer. The pieces scattered all over the land.

And that is why, to this day, there are many drums and drummers all over Haiti.

Anansi Tricks Three Kings

This story is based on a folk tale from St Vincent

Once upon a time there was a king and in his kingdom there was a drought. In the king's garden there was a well, and this well provided all the fresh water for the village.

The people of the village needed permission from the king to get water from the well, and they all relied on the fresh water to live. Without it they would all die. This made the king very powerful indeed.

Brer Anansi was very jealous of the king. You see, Brer Anansi didn't like the fact that the king had all the power. Brer Anansi wanted to be the all-powerful one instead. Now everyone knows how Brer Anansi is a trickster and, since days gone by, Brer Anansi has been known to outsmart the mightiest of people. So Brer Anansi thought for a long time about how he could outsmart the king.

Then Brer Anansi had an idea. Every night when the king was sleeping, Brer Anansi decided he would sneak into the king's garden and drain some of the water away from the well. Since the water in the well was what made the king powerful, he would get rid of it so that the king would lose his power over the people.

And that's exactly what he did. Night after night, little by little, Brer Anansi emptied the water in the well until there was hardly any left. When the king went to the well and saw that nearly all the water had gone he was very suspicious.

'Somebody is emptying my well,' he said. 'I will find the culprit and make him pay!'

The king decided to set a trap for the thief. He made a man out of tar and put the man next to the well. He put a piece of bread in one hand and a fish in the other to make the tar man look like he was a real man, taking a meal. The king was sure that the thief would stop and try and talk to the tar man, and eventually he would think he was being ignored and would start a fight with the tar man. That was the plan.

Well, just as the king had thought, Brer Anansi came that night to get the last bit of water in the well. When he arrived and saw the man standing next to the well, Brer Anansi said, 'Howdi.' Of course, the tar man didn't answer. So Brer Anansi said a little louder, 'I said, Howdi!' but there still was no reply. 'Fella, I'm talking to you!' said Brer Anansi, vexed now. Still there was no answer.

Now Brer Anansi has a bit of a temper and gets upset when he thinks anyone is being rude to him, so he put his head right next to the tar face and said, 'Who are you, anyway? The king's watchman? You're going on like you think you are so great, but you are no better than I am!'

Still the man did not answer, so Brer Anansi threw a punch right at his face. But because tar is sticky, Brer Anansi's hand stuck there, right in the tar man's jaw.

'Get off my hand!' said Brer Anansi, and he grabbed the tar man with his other hand. As he did so, of course, his other hand got stuck too.

By now Brer Anansi was even more angry, so he raised up his knee to push the man over, but as his knee hit the belly of the tar man it too stuck fast. This was all too much for Brer Anansi and he pushed himself on the man, trying to toss him into the well. The more he wrestled with the tar man, the more Brer Anansi stuck, until he was fastened completely and could not move at all.

The next morning the king went to see if his plan had worked and he saw Brer Anansi stuck fast to the tar man.

'Brer Anansi!' said the king. 'I should have known it was you!'

The king was very pleased that he had caught Brer Anansi. He told his servants to chain Anansi up until he could think of a suitable punishment for him.

Later that day, still unsure of the best punishment, the king had his men bring Brer Anansi to him.

'I will make sure you suffer for stealing water from my well!' said the king. 'Maybe I should burn you on a coal fire.'

Brer Anansi said nothing. The king watched carefully for a reaction, but Brer Anansi remained silent.

'Or maybe I should whip you!' said the king. Still Brer Anansi said nothing.

'Or perhaps I should drown you in the sea!' said the king.

'Oh no, please don't drown me in the sea!' cried Brer Anansi. 'You can do anything else to me, but please don't drown me in the sea!'

When the king heard Brer Anansi's pleas not to drown him, he thought that this would be the best punishment.

The king and two of his guards took Brer Anansi out on a boat, tied a rope around his waist with some heavy iron on the other end and, when the boat got to the middle of the ocean, they threw Brer Anansi overboard into the water.

Brer Anansi immediately sank right down to the bottom of the ocean. But once at the bottom, Brer Anansi untied the rope from his waist, and he floated right back up to the top of the water.

'We spiders always float back up!' laughed Brer Anansi. 'You did me a favour!' he called out to the king. 'You may be a king but I am much smarter than you are!'

Then Brer Anansi dived back down into the water, where he saw a shark. It seemed that all the little creatures in the sea, the fishes, the lobsters and the crabs, were afraid of the shark.

'Who is that?' said Brer Anansi. 'And why are you all so afraid of him?'

'That's our king,' said the sea creatures. 'He's powerful! If we get in his way he eats us up!'

'Well, I don't care for kings much' said Brer Anansi. 'I'm smarter than all of them! I've already made a fool out of one.'

The small fish trembled. 'Well, King Shark is the most powerful in all of the sea. You would be better off if you kept out of his way.'

Saying that to Brer Anansi only got him angry.

'We'll see about that!' said Brer Anansi. And he swam right over to King Shark and he said, 'King Shark, I have been looking for you for such a long time.'

King Shark was not impressed with Brer Anansi's casual approach. 'How dare you speak to me, you incey wincey thing! Do you know who I am? I am the all-powerful king! Out of my way, before I eat you!'

Brer Anansi ducked out of the ferocious King Shark's way, just as he was about to snap him up in his jaws, and he shouted from a safe distance, 'Sorry to disturb you. It's just that I wanted to invite you to a feast, but if you're busy . . .'

'You're inviting me to a feast?' interrupted King Shark, suddenly interested. 'What kind of a feast?'

'A tasty fish feast!' said Brer Anansi, getting a little closer to King Shark now that he had his attention. 'If you help me catch the fish, we can cook them up and have a tasty feast this afternoon.'

'Cooked fish!' sniggered King Shark, intrigued. 'That will make a change from eating them raw. I'll come to your feast!'

'Fine. First we have to catch the fish!' said Brer Anansi, glad that he had managed to convince King Shark to join him.

'Oh, that's easy enough!' snapped King Shark, and he cut through the water at great speed. The little fish tried to get away but King Shark was too fast for them and he caught plenty.

When it was time to bring the fish ashore, Brer Anansi called to King Shark, 'Come ashore, King Shark! Come ashore!'

'I'll stay in the water while you cook up the fish,' said King Shark. 'I can only stay out of the water for a couple of minutes so you cook them up and bring me my share when you're done.'

Brer Anansi agreed to cook up the fish and then bring King Shark his share, while King Shark waited in the water.

Brer Anansi fetched some wood and lit a fire, ready to cook the fish. He put a big copper pot full of water on the fire and he filled the pot of water with the fish they had caught. When the fish were all cooked up in the water and steaming hot, Brer Anansi called to King Shark, 'King Shark! Come ashore and join me for the feast! I've heard you can stand on the tip of your tail! Show me.'

Well, King Shark liked to show off, so he was ready to come out of the water without much persuasion.

'I will,' said King Shark, 'but only for half a minute, otherwise I will die in the sun.'

And as King Shark came out of the water and stood up on the tip of his tail, Brer Anansi pretended he was impressed.

'That's amazing! I have never seen a shark stand up on the tip of its tail!'

'Well, I'm the all-powerful king,' King Shark boasted. 'I can do anything!'

As King Shark showed off with his balancing antics, Brer Anansi thought he would take this moment to destroy him, so he used a bucket to take out some of the steaming water. He threw it at King Shark and killed him right where he stood, balancing on his tail! Once King Shark was lying on the ground, Brer Anansi laughed and cut him up into pieces. He put him in the copper pot to boil with the rest of the fish.

'You may be a king,' said Brer Anansi, 'but I am much smarter than you are!'

Feeling pleased with himself, Brer Anansi added some peppers and allowed all the fish to cook up well. There was much too much fish to eat by himself, but he didn't care. He was a greedy and selfish spider and he was happy to throw away what he couldn't manage to eat.

But Brer Anansi wasn't alone. As he cooked his fish supper he saw King Lion creep up on him. King Lion had smelt the sweet aroma of Brer Anansi's cooking and he wanted to have some.

Brer Anansi was afraid, but he didn't let King Lion know this. 'Ah, King Lion, you are just the man I wanted to see,' said Brer Anansi. 'I have a fish feast here, more than enough for me. Will you help me eat it?'

'Mmm, gladly,' growled King Lion. King Lion licked his lips and made himself comfortable, as Brer Anansi finished preparing the food. When the fish feast was ready King Lion could hardly wait to get started. For every fish Brer Anansi ate, King Lion ate six fishes. Brer Anansi was furious that he had done all the hard work and King Lion was eating the most.

He grumbled, 'It's not fair! I caught the fish, I made the

fire, I carried the big copper pot to the stove and cooked all the fish, and yet you've eaten more fish than I have!'

'You'd better stop your grumbling,' roared King Lion, 'or I might just eat you up too!'

Brer Anansi shut up at once. He was very afraid of what King Lion might do, so he thought it best to keep quiet. He didn't say anything while they ate but he thought a lot about how to get his own back.

When they had finished eating, Brer Anansi said, 'Remember the game we used to play at school?'

Now Brer Anansi and King Lion had gone to the same school when they were young, when Brer Anansi was tiny and King Lion was just a little lion cub.

'I don't remember any game!' said King Lion.

Brer Anansi said, 'I'll remind you. We take a little piece of string and you put your two hands behind your back and I tie you up to a tree. Then I take a small twig and I just lightly touch your back with it. Then you break out of the string and get away and then you do the same to me.'

'Oh,' said King Lion, 'well, I don't remember this game at all, but I don't mind playing it with you – as long as I get to tie you up first!'

'That's fine with me,' said Brer Anansi.

So King Lion took the little piece of string and he tied Brer Anansi to the tree, then he took a small twig and lightly touched Brer Anansi's back with it.

'He-he-he, that tickles,' laughed Brer Anansi and he broke out of the string and got away.

'Your turn now, King Lion!' said Brer Anansi, and King Lion got ready to be tied to the tree.

But this time, instead of using a little piece of string, Brer Anansi took a thick cord rope out of his pocket and he tied King Lion to the tree tightly. Then, instead of a small twig, Brer Anansi took a large branch from the tree and whipped it across King Lion's back, hard. King Lion immediately tried to pull away, but the rope held him firmly to the tree. Brer Anansi hit him again with the tree branch, then again and again. He beat King Lion over and over until King Lion was half dead and then Brer Anansi left King Lion on the ground.

'Serves you right!' laughed Brer Anansi. 'You ate all my fish! You didn't think I was going to let you get away with it, did you? You may be a king,' shouted Brer Anansi, 'but I am much smarter than you are!' and Brer Anansi ran off home.

'I'm smarter than three kings!' laughed Brer Anansi.

King Lion was all battered and bruised. He was trying to work out how to untie himself when he saw a lady walking by.

'Please, Ma'am,' he pleaded, 'please can you untie me? Else I will surely die.'

The lady was afraid at first. 'Who tied you and left you there?' she asked.

'Brer Anansi did this to me!' said King Lion. 'He asked me to play a game we used to play at school with him. I tied him up first and he broke the string, like we used to do at school, and he got away. But then he had to tie me and instead of using the same little string, he used a much stronger cord rope. He tied me to this tree and then he beat me with a big tree branch until I was half dead!'

'That's terrible,' said the lady. 'But you're King Lion, the most ferocious animal around. If I untie you, how do I know you will not eat me?'

'If I try to eat you, all the trees and stones around here will cry "shame"!'

So the lady agreed to untie King Lion. As she did so, King Lion tried to eat her all up! But just as he had said, all the trees and the stones round about cried out, 'Shame, Lion! Shame!'

King Lion immediately stopped and let the lady go.

Ashamed of himself for letting Brer Anansi catch him and then breaking his word with the lady, King Lion went home and told his wife what had happened.

'You must get your own back on Anansi!' King Lion's wife said. 'You are much stronger than him, but that spider is full of tricks and mischief. Don't worry, we will think of a way to get back at him.'

So King Lion and his wife thought all night about how they could get Brer Anansi back. They thought and thought until eventually King Lion's wife had an idea.

'We'll have a party. You know how Brer Anansi likes to dance. We'll invite everyone to come along, apart from him! You know Brer Anansi, he'll find a way to be there. And once he is in our home, we will trap him and kill him.'

'That sounds like a fine plan,' said King Lion.

Just as King Lion and his wife had planned, Brer Anansi heard about how everybody else had been invited to King Lion's party and he didn't want to miss out. He decided he would go to the party in disguise. So he told his wife to wrap him up in a white sheet and asked her to carry him to the dance as if he was a baby. He told her that if anyone should recognize who he was then she should just throw him out of the window in the sheet.

The party was in full swing when they arrived. King Lion and his wife were looking around at the guests, to see if Brer Anansi had arrived, when King Lion's wife noticed that Brer Anansi's wife was at the party, and carrying a very large baby! Of course, they knew straight away that it was bound to be Brer Anansi.

King Lion pulled on the sheet and at once Brer Anansi called out to his wife, 'Quick, use the sheet to throw me out of the window!'

But the party music was so sweet and Brer Anansi's wife was having such a good time dancing that she didn't take any notice.

Brer Anansi had to try and escape all by himself. He

ran and he ran, with King Lion running right behind him. He ran until he saw a crab hole next to a pepper tree. He grabbed some peppers, put them in his mouth, crushed them, and then jumped into the hole. King Lion came to the hole and dug down until it was big enough for him to see Brer Anansi. But just as he saw him, Brer Anansi spat out the peppers, right into King Lion's eyes! It hurt the lion's eyes so much, he couldn't see.

'Ouch! Ouch! Ouch!' cried King Lion. While he was crying in pain, Brer Anansi took the opportunity to bop him on the head and finish him off. King Lion fell down dead and Brer Anansi chopped him up into pieces and carried him home in his bag. When he got home he put Lion in a pot to make lion soup.

And that is how Brer Anansi outsmarted three kings!

The Special Pumpkin

This story is based on a folk tale from Martinique

Maman was old and she knew it. Her hair was thinning and what was left of it was grey. Her body ached and she could hardly walk. Her husband had died many years before, and her sons, their wives and their children had moved away from Martinique to live in far-off countries.

Maman had no visitors, save her greedy neighbour, Madame Jalousie. Madame Jalousie would only pass by Maman's house to show off about how good her life was and to tell Maman how well her own children were doing and how often they visited her.

Madame Jalousie liked to brag about all sorts of things. Often she would brag to Maman about all the different vegetables she had growing in her garden. She knew well that Maman's garden no longer bore fruit or vegetables. Watercress was the only thing that grew in Maman's garden these days.

Maman just listened to Madame Jalousie with an open heart and never asked for anything. Madame Jalousie never offered Maman anything either, even though she knew that all Maman had to eat was wild watercress.

So Maman ate watercress stew, watercress soup, watercress pie and watercress cake, and she dreamed of all the wonderful fruits and vegetables she used to eat when she was younger, when her garden was full. Maman would dream about eating a juicy mango and sucking the pulp right down to the seed, or eating sour sop or breadfruit, or even a hearty chicken stew with dumplings, or fried fish and johnnycakes. But Maman never grumbled. Instead she rejoiced. Maman had had a full and joyous life with her family and she had many fond memories. So when Madame Jalousie visited Maman empty-handed, Maman just smiled and wished her neighbour well.

One day Maman was sitting on her verandah when a tiny, beautiful bird landed at her feet. The bird's wings had some feathers the colour of the turquoise blue sea, and some feathers the colour of a warm orange sunset.

'What a beautiful bird!' she said to herself. 'And how lovely that you have chosen to spend a moment with me.'

But when the old lady looked closer at the bird, she noticed that one of the wings on the bird was broken. Feeling sorry for the bird, Maman picked it up carefully so as not to hurt its fragile body and tenderly put it against her chest to keep it safe and warm.

'There, there . . .' she said. 'Now don't you worry, I'll take care of you.' And that was what Maman did. Every day she gave the bird clean water to drink and shared with it her watercress. She kept the bird safe, away from harm, and she grew to love it with all her heart. She sang to it every day:

> 'Bel oiseau, bel oiseau,
> Je vais vous faire forte,'

which means:

> 'Beautiful bird, beautiful bird,
> I will make you strong.'

Slowly, slowly, the bird began to get stronger and stronger, and gradually the broken wing began to heal. Finally, one day, the bird's wing was well enough for it to fly again. Maman watched the bird fly around her all day long and finally she decided that it was time to let the bird go. The old lady had enjoyed the company, but she knew that the best thing for the bird was to let it fly out into the sky. So one day she put the bird on the palm of her hand and said,

'Allez, petit oiseau,'

which means,

'Go, little bird.'

And the bird flew away, up into the sky, gently flapping its wings.

With the bird gone, Maman was once again alone, except from the occasional visits from her greedy neighbour, Madame Jalousie. Maman would often look up to the sky to see if her friend, the beautiful blue and orange bird, was passing, but it never came back. Maman didn't grumble. She was thankful that she had shared a lovely time with the bird and she enjoyed the memory.

Then, to Maman's surprise, one day as she was sitting watching the sun come up, she heard the gently flapping wings above her head. When she looked up, it was none other than the beautiful blue and orange bird that she had nursed. She was so glad that the bird had come back.

But the bird had not come to stay. Instead, it dropped something from its beak and flew away again. The old lady was sad to see it fly away so quickly, but she looked on the ground to see what it had left her and there, at her feet, lay a small pumpkin seed.

'Oh, a pumpkin seed!' said Maman. 'Thank you. I will plant the seed in my garden.'

Maman took the seed to the bottom of her garden and she planted the seed very carefully in the soil. Every day she watered her pumpkin seed and talked and sang to it:

> *'Petite graine, petite graine,*
> *Je vais vous faire forte,'*

which means:

> *'Little seed, little seed,*
> *I will make you strong.'*

And, as the sun shone on the seed, after a few days the seed began to sprout. Maman was so excited when she saw the tiny shoot that she began to sing to it even more sweetly than before:

> *'Petite graine, petite graine,*
> *Je vais vous faire forte.*
>
> *Little seed, little seed,*
> *I will make you strong.'*

Before long the shoot grew into a vine that began to flower. Maman loved her pumpkin plant and she encouraged it to grow. And, soon enough, a pumpkin did begin to grow. Maman loved her pumpkin and sang even more sweetly than before.

While she waited for the pumpkin to ripen, Maman imagined all the dishes she would be able to make – pumpkin soup, fried pumpkin, roast pumpkin, grilled pumpkin, pumpkin stew, pumpkin pie . . . She couldn't wait to taste it.

At last the day finally arrived and the pumpkin was ripe. Maman's mouth watered as she brought it inside to carve it up.

But when Maman sliced the pumpkin, a strange thing happened.

Inside, instead of the pumpkin flesh and seeds she expected, it was filled with all of Maman's favourite dishes from the days when she used to eat with her family. There was a hearty chicken stew with dumplings, and fried fish and johnnycakes. There was breadfruit and sour sop and the flesh of the juiciest mango. Maman could not believe her eyes! She ate and ate and ate until her belly was so full it felt like it was about to burst. There was still plenty of food left in the pumpkin.

'So much food!' Maman said. 'Much too much for me alone, I will take some to my neighbour.' And that is what Maman did. She wrapped the rest of the special pumpkin in paper and brought it to Madame Jalousie.

'I have brought you some food from my very special pumpkin,' said Maman. Madame Jalousie tore open the paper. When she saw all the food inside, she ate greedily without so much as a thank you. But Maman wasn't expecting any thanks from Madame Jalousie, so it didn't make any difference to her. Maman was only glad that the food in the pumpkin wasn't going to go to waste.

Maman went home and, before she went to bed, she thought about how the little bird had been so kind to bring her the pumpkin seed, and she was thankful for her blessings.

The next day, when Maman woke up and looked out into her garden, she found a wondrous surprise. There in the garden was another ripe pumpkin! Maman was so excited, and once again when she cut the pumpkin open she saw it was full of even more of her favourite food. There was saltfish, oxtail stew and souse. There was sweet potato and christophine and the sweetest passion fruit. Maman was so happy. Once again she had been provided with a feast of a meal. Maman ate and ate and ate until her belly was so full it felt like it was about to burst. Still there was plenty of food left in the pumpkin.

'I'll bring the rest for Madame Jalousie,' Maman said and, just as before, she wrapped the remainder in some paper and brought it to her neighbour. When Madame Jalousie saw Maman approaching, she ran out to her and snatched the food from her hands.

'The pumpkin you brought yesterday was so nice!' she said greedily, and ate up all the food without a word of thanks to Maman. Maman left Madame Jalousie stuffing the food in her mouth and smiled. She was just glad that the food was not going to be wasted.

The next day when Maman woke up there was yet another pumpkin in her garden, filled with more of her favourite foods. After eating enough to fill her belly, Maman brought Madame Jalousie the rest. But this time, as Madame Jalousie ate greedily from the pumpkin, she stopped Maman from leaving and said, 'You must tell me how it is that you get to grow such special pumpkins!'

And Maman told her how the beautiful blue and orange bird had appeared in her garden with the broken wing. She told her how she had nursed the bird and how, when the wing was better, she had let the bird fly away. She told Madame Jalousie that the bird had come back and left her the pumpkin seed, and how she had planted the seed and cared for it, and how the pumpkin had grown ripe and she had cut it open to find all the food she loved.

'Then I will get a pumpkin, just like yours!' said Madame Jalousie.

The next day Madame Jalousie sat on her verandah, looking up at the sky to see if a blue and orange bird would fly to her too. The sky remained clear. When Maman came with the special pumpkin food to give her, as she had done before, Madame Jalousie said, 'Go away! I don't want your leftovers! I am going to have my own pumpkin!'

Every day Madame Jalousie looked in the sky for the blue and orange bird, but it was nowhere to be seen.

And then, finally, to Madame Jalousie's delight, one day a beautiful blue and orange bird landed on the fence of her verandah. As the bird was about to fly away again, Madame Jalousie grabbed it. Without a moment's thought she twisted the bird's wing until it snapped. The poor bird shrieked with pain. Then Madame Jalousie threw it into a dark corner of her room. She threw some scraps of food after it.

'Hurry up and get better!' she said. 'I want my pumpkin!'

With no love in her heart Madame Jalousie checked on the bird every day to see if the wing was better, but it would not heal.

'Hurry up and get better!' she said. 'I want my pumpkin!'

Madame Jalousie became tired of waiting and after three days she took the bird outside and said,

'Allez-vous en! Allez-vous en!'

which means,

'Go away! Go away!'

The poor bird tried to leave but it could hardly fly on its broken wing.

'*Volez, oiseau!*' Madame Jalousie said. 'Fly away, bird!'

And she picked up the bird and threw it out. The bird tried with all its might to fly and eventually flapped the good wing so hard that it could fly away from the evil woman. As the bird flew away Madame Jalousie shouted after it, 'Hurry up! I want my pumpkin!'

Well, weeks and weeks went by and there was no sign of the bird with the pumpkin seed. Madame Jalousie grew more and more impatient.

'Where is that stupid bird!' she moaned. 'I want a pumpkin seed just like Maman's. I want a pumpkin with food in it, just like Maman's!'

But there was still no sign of the bird with the seed and Madame Jalousie grew more and more vexed.

'That stupid bird is never coming back!' she said angrily. 'I hope it is dead!'

And as she said that, the sky grew dark and thunder began to rumble in the sky. That night there was a terrible storm. The next day, when Madame Jalousie went out on to her verandah, she heard the sound of gently flapping wings above her head. Lo and behold, when she looked up she saw the blue and orange bird had returned.

'Looks like your wing has got better then!' Madame

Jalousie said, without any care. 'Now where's my pumpkin seed? Give it to me!'

The bird dropped something from its beak and flew away again. Madame Jalousie was glad to see the back of the bird and called and jeered as it flew away.

'About time! And good riddance!' she shouted, and then she bent down to pick up her pumpkin seed.

'Hooray! Now I can plant my seed and get my pumpkin!' she said ungratefully. She put the seed in her garden, paying no mind to where she planted it. She did not care for it at all. All she was bothered about was getting a pumpkin.

'Seed! Hurry up and grow!' she shouted. 'I want my pumpkin!'

Eventually the seed began to sprout. Madame Jalousie grew more restless.

'What's taking so long?' she shouted. 'Hurry up, I want my pumpkin *now*!'

After some time the shoot grew into a vine, which began to flower, but still Madame Jalousie grew more and more restless.

'I want my pumpkin!' she shouted. 'I want my pumpkin!'

Slowly, slowly, the pumpkin grew, but Madame Jalousie knew that she could not have it until it was ripe.

'Hurry up and ripen, you stupid pumpkin!' she shouted. 'You're taking too long!'

At last the day finally arrived when Madame Jalousie's pumpkin was ripe. Madame Jalousie took up a machete and she cut into the pumpkin.

But to her horror when she looked inside, instead of all the lovely food that Maman had found, Madame Jalousie's pumpkin was filled with spiders and cockroaches and mosquitos and scorpions!

'Euuuuuuugggghhhh!' cried Madame Jalousie. 'Where's my food? I want food in my pumpkin, like Maman!' But there was no food to be found, only creepy-crawlies.

Madame Jalousie was so disgusted at what she saw that she ran away from all the nasty creatures coming out of her pumpkin and she was never seen again.

As for Maman, she lived the rest of her days enjoying the delicious food from all of the special pumpkins that grew in her garden.

The Singing Turtle

This story is based on a folk tale from Haiti

There was once a turtle who loved to sing. It was not something that she did in public as this would have drawn attention to her gift – and Turtle was a very private creature. She enjoyed plodding along steadily without a fuss and she was happy to watch others take the limelight.

The truth was, Turtle knew that if anyone were to learn about her secret it would be very dangerous for her. She feared that she might be captured and put in a cage or a museum or science laboratory. Singing out loud wasn't worth the risk. Turtle much preferred the quiet life and so she only sang in secret. Most days she would sing quietly to herself as she took her long slow walks. On other days when Turtle knew that no one was around, she would sing loudly at the top of her voice. She loved those days best, because on those days Turtle could let go and be herself. Yes, on those days Turtle could allow her songs to flow and she would sing whatever came to her mind.

'I love to sing,
I love to sing,
More than anything,
I love to sing.'

One day, as Turtle was plodding along, she thought she was alone and was singing at the top of her voice. Suddenly she heard someone cheering and clapping. When she turned to see who had been listening she saw a flock of birds. There were nightingales, pigeons, chickens, ducks, seagulls – all kinds of birds. They were all clapping their wings together in appreciation of Turtle's fine song.

'Fabulous!' cried the nightingales.

'Encore!' cried the ducks.

'What a beautiful voice!' cried the pigeons.

Then the birds went back to eating the peas and millet that a nearby farmer had planted in his field.

'Come and join us,' the pigeons called to Turtle.

'There's plenty here for all of us to enjoy,' the chickens clucked.

'Come and eat with us!' cried the nightingales.

But Turtle wasn't interested in trespassing on the farmer's land or in attracting any more attention to herself. She knew that should the farmer come out and catch the birds they would soon fly away, but she would not be able to move so quickly and she would be caught.

'It's all right,' Turtle said, 'I'm not hungry.' And she went on her way.

The next day Turtle was walking the same way and she saw the birds again, eating all the peas and millet on the farmer's land. They noticed her passing and called again.

'You really will enjoy this!' the seagulls called.

'Tasty stuff!' quacked the ducks.

'Come get your belly full!' the turkeys said.

But even though the food looked good Turtle just walked on by. She was not prepared to take the risk.

'Not today,' she said, and just plodded along.

Well, on the third day, when Turtle saw all the birds eating the peas and millet on the farmer's land, she began to think that maybe she might be able to get a little to eat without being caught. After all, on all the days she had passed the birds, she had not once seen any sign of the farmer.

'Well, are you coming?' asked the pigeons.

'The thing is,' said Turtle, 'I'm not a very fast mover, and if the farmer comes out you all have wings and you can fly away. I don't and the farmer will be sure to catch me.'

'Then we'll give you some wings,' said the birds, and each one of the birds attached one of their fine feathers to Turtle's shell.

'Thank you very much!' said Turtle, and she went into the field to join them.

Turtle ate and ate with the birds until her belly was full. But, alas, while they were eating the nightingale called out, 'The farmer is coming! Fly! Fly!' And, in a panic, the birds quickly grabbed the feathers they had given to Turtle and flew away. Turtle was left stranded. She tried to get away, but because her little legs crawled so slowly the farmer caught her.

'Ahhhhh, you little rascal!' the farmer said angrily. 'So you and your feathered friends think you can get away with stealing my crop, do you? Well, I'm going to make you pay for it!' And, just as the farmer was about to beat Turtle, full of fear she began to sing:

> 'If I could fly,
> I'd fly away,
> But sad to say
> I have no wings.'

When the farmer heard Turtle sing, he could not believe what he was hearing.

'Sing for me again!' he said, and Turtle sang again:

> *'If I could fly,*
> *I'd fly away,*
> *But sad to say*
> *I have no wings.*
>
> *I love to sing,*
> *I love to sing,*
> *More than anything,*
> *I love to sing.'*

'A singing turtle?' said the farmer. 'What a catch! You could make me very rich!'

The farmer brought Turtle home with him and he put her in a box until he could think of the best way to make money out of her. The box was dark and cold and Turtle was very afraid. If only she had listened to her first instinct and not gone into the farmer's field, she would be safe now!

That night the farmer did not sleep at all. All through the night he kept thinking about how rich the singing turtle could make him and, the more he thought about it, the more greedy and restless he became. The farmer's wife asked him what was keeping him awake, but the man didn't like his wife very much and he was very greedy. So he didn't tell her about the singing turtle as he wanted to keep all the money he would make for himself.

'Nothing for you to worry about, my dear wife,' he said. 'You go back to sleep.'

But the farmer's wife knew that her husband was up to something. 'Are you sure there is nothing you want to tell me?' she said.

'I am sure,' said the farmer.

The next day, when the farmer got out of bed, he knew exactly what he was going to do. He put some grass and some water in the box for the turtle, so she could eat and drink while he was away, and then he hid the box under his bed. He put on his suit.

'Where are you going?' said the farmer's wife.

'I have some business to do in town,' said the farmer, and he set off to Port-au-Prince.

Once there, he told everyone he met about his singing turtle, until gradually word got around and all those with money wanted to buy it. The farmer, however, would not sell until he found the person who had the most money. When the president heard about the singing turtle he came to the farmer. The farmer thought his luck was in and was waiting to hear how much the president was prepared to pay, but the president didn't believe that the farmer was telling the truth.

'There is no such thing as a singing turtle,' said the

president. 'You are nothing but a cheat and a liar! And for that you will be punished.'

'I am telling the truth!' said the farmer. 'And I will sell the singing turtle to the highest bidder. Come to my house and see for yourself. If I am lying, you can punish me!' So the president and all the people followed the farmer back to his home.

Meanwhile, the farmer's wife had been wondering what her husband was up to. She searched high and low for the box she had seen her husband with, to see if that could help her find out what he was hiding from her. She imagined that it was probably a box of money since she knew how greedy he was. She told herself that if she was to find it she would keep the money for herself and leave him with none. The farmer's wife finally searched in the bedroom and found the box under the bed.

'Got it!' she said happily. 'Now I am a rich lady.' When the farmer's wife opened the box she was very disappointed.

'An ugly old turtle!' she said. 'Is that all!'

The farmer's wife was about to put the lid back on the box and put it back under the bed when the turtle said, 'No, don't put me back! Please! I'm not just any old turtle. I'm a singing turtle!'

'A singing turtle?' said the farmer's wife. 'That could make me very rich! Go ahead, then, let me hear you sing!'

Turtle thought a while. She had to be very smart if she was to get away.

'I can only sing by the edge of the river,' said Turtle.

'Very well,' said the farmer's wife, 'I will take you there.' So the farmer's wife carried the box with Turtle in it to the river's edge.

'There you go,' she said. 'Now sing for me.'

Turtle knew she had to be very smart if she was to escape, so she said, 'I can only sing when my feet are wet.'

'Very well,' said the farmer's wife, taking Turtle out of the box and placing her in the water by the bank of the river. Turtle crawled into the water quickly and swam away.

'Oh no!' cried the farmer's wife. 'You tricked me!'

Just then, the farmer's wife heard her husband's voice. 'This way! This way!' she heard him say, and as she looked in the distance she could see him leading a crowd of people to her house.

He must be bringing them to see the singing turtle, she thought. *I must do something!*

Afraid of what her husband might do, the farmer's wife found a lizard, which she quickly put in the box. She put the lid on the box, then ran as fast as she could back to the house. The farmer's wife managed to get back to the house before her husband arrived with the crowd, and slipped the box back under the bed. The farmer marched to the bedroom and triumphantly took out the box from under his bed to show to the crowd.

'Inside this box,' said the farmer, 'is the most amazing

reptile.' And without opening the box the farmer said, 'Sing, Turtle, sing!'

The lizard replied from inside the box, 'Cric!'

The crowd began to laugh and the president looked angry. The farmer tapped the box and said again, 'Sing, Turtle, sing!'

And the lizard replied, 'Crac!'

This time the crowd laughed louder and the president became angrier. 'What foolishness is this?' said the president. 'Remember I warned you that you will be punished if there is no singing turtle!'

The farmer's wife, knowing what she had done, decided to slip out of the house at that moment. She could see that the president was not at all pleased and she did not want to be part of the punishment her husband was going to get.

'One moment,' said the farmer, lifting the lid from the box. To his horror, there inside the box was a lizard instead of the turtle. 'But this can't be!' said the farmer.

'You cheat!' said the president, and turning to two men in the crowd he said, 'Take this man down to the river to be drowned!'

'NO! NO!' screamed the farmer. 'There's been a mistake. Someone has stolen my singing turtle!'

But nobody listened to the farmer. Two men marched him down to the river, as the president had ordered. When they reached the river and the farmer was just about to be thrown into the water, Turtle stuck her head out of the water and sang:

> 'Farmer, eh!
> If you could fly away,
> But sad to say
> You have no wings.'

'That's her!' said the farmer. 'That's my singing Turtle! Listen to her sing!' And the Turtle carried on singing:

> 'President, eh!
> The farmer talk too much!
> May he learn from this,
> Now set him free!'

When the president heard the singing turtle, he set the farmer free. And from that day the farmer was never so quick to open his big mouth to tell secrets any more, and the singing turtle hid herself away and was never seen again.

The Girl with the Star on her Head

This story is based on a folk tale from Haiti

It is said that some babies are born with stars on their foreheads. It is said that some babies get the stars when they are older. These stars are invisible to the ordinary human eye, but they are there nonetheless. Not even the child who has a star on her forehead knows that it is there because it is invisible. These stars, I am told, are put on the child to mark them for extra protection. If something bad is going to happen to them, the star finds a way to protect them.

Amalie was such a child, born with an invisible star on her forehead.

Now Amalie's mother had died when she was still a baby and that left her father to look after her. Amalie's father was worried, as he didn't think he was very good at doing all the things he had seen his wife do with the baby: feeding her and rocking her to sleep.

But when he held Amalie the love oozed out of him and she felt as comfortable in his arms as she had in her mother's. Amalie's father was still afraid that his daughter might miss out on important things if he did not marry again, however. So he quickly became engaged to someone new so that his daughter could have a mother in her life. Although Amalie's father was doing what he thought was right, the woman he chose to be Amalie's stepmother wasn't someone who had Amalie's best interests at heart. Amalie's stepmother had two daughters of her own, and they were spoilt and greedy. When they met Amalie and saw how beautiful she was, both inside and out, they were extremely jealous of her and treated her badly.

In front of her father they would speak sweetly about Amalie, but whenever they were alone with their mother they would say, 'Mummy, why must we share a bedroom with that ugly wretch?'

And their mother would reply, 'It won't be forever. We'll soon get rid of her!'

One day Amalie's father was offered work in a far-off land, a job that would give him lots and lots of money. But it would mean him spending a lot of time away from home. Though they needed the money (as his new wife didn't work) Amalie's father did not want to leave his family, so he asked his wife what he should do.

'Of course you should take the job!' said his wife, for she was a greedy woman and cared not that she would barely see her husband. And so take it he did. It was a sad day for Amalie when her father left because she loved him so dearly. She also knew how her stepsisters hated her and how her stepmother only treated her well when her father was around. Without him at home life for her would be very different.

And she was right.

As soon as Amalie's father left, Amalie's stepmother and her daughters began to whisper to each other and giggle, all the time looking over at Amalie.

'Mummy, you promised that you would get rid of her!' said one daughter.

'Yes, Mummy, when will that be?' asked the other.

'Soon . . .' said Amalie's stepmother.

Amalie's father worked very hard while he was away and he sent lots of money to his new wife so that she could take care of the home and the family. But she only looked after herself and her own daughters. She bought them pretty dresses and jewellery and she bought nothing for Amalie, who wore only rags.

One day Amalie's stepmother made a visit to an evil wizard in the nearby town and told him she wanted to get rid of her stepdaughter. Now the evil wizard was happy to do this as he was a wicked man through and through.

'Very well, madam!' he said. 'I will come at midnight, marking my arrival with the sound of a cock crowing, and I will take your stepdaughter away. Be sure to leave her outside for me to collect as I cannot come indoors to get her. My powers only work outside.'

So that was the arrangement. Amalie's stepmother was to leave Amalie outside the house at midnight, like a bag of rubbish, and the evil wizard would collect her and take her away. Amalie's stepmother told her daughters about the plan, and they told Amalie nothing.

Now Amalie didn't trust any of them, but she had to live with them, so she tried to get on with them the best she could. She suspected they were probably up to something but she didn't know what.

'Amalie!' called one of the stepsisters. 'Let's play a game!'

This was unusual for a start, as neither of the stepsisters liked to play with Amalie.

'What would you like to play?' Amalie asked cautiously.

'Hide and seek!' said the other stepsister. They had already discussed their plan with each other.

Amalie didn't want to be unfriendly so she agreed to play hide and seek with them.

'We'll hide and you seek us out!' said the sisters.

Amalie agreed.

'But first let's go outside,' they said. 'There's not enough room in the house. There's nowhere for us to hide inside.' So Amalie and the stepsisters went outside.

'Close your eyes and count to ten,' they told her, and Amalie did so. As soon as they saw that Amalie's eyes were closed, Amalie's stepsisters ran straight back to the house and went inside, locking the door behind them. When she had finished counting, Amalie opened her eyes and began to look for her stepsisters in the street. Of course they were nowhere to be found. Amalie looked and called out for them until night-time, but still she couldn't find them anywhere. Meanwhile, her stepsisters were snuggled up in bed, caring nothing for her safety.

As it got later and later, Amalie got frightened. She did not like the dark very much because she knew that was when witches and wizards came out, but she was worried for her stepsisters and didn't want to leave them outside. She carried on searching for them but still, of course, she could not find them. Finally, she gave up and decided to go home to ask for her stepmother's help. It was almost midnight when she reached her door. But try as she might, the door was shut fast. Amalie knocked loudly but no one came to answer.

Just then a cockerel crowed, 'Cock-a-doodle-doo! Cock-a-doodle-doo!' and the evil wizard jumped out from the darkness. Amalie was startled and started to scream. All of a sudden, the star on her forehead began to glow.

'I've come to take you away!' said the wizard, reaching out to grab her. But, as he did so, something very like a laser beam shot out and knocked him all the way into the next district. The wizard didn't know what had hit him!

Amalie was in shock. She turned and knocked on her front door even louder than before, shouting for her stepmother to open it.

'Stepmother! Stepmother! Open the door! An evil wizard is trying to take me away!'

But the stepmother just laughed and turned over in her sleep.

'No, I won't open the door! If the evil wizard wants you, he can keep you!' she said.

'Stepmother! Stepmother! Open the door!' called Amalie again.

'Child, go and trouble your father and leave me alone!' shouted her stepmother.

Amalie didn't know what to do. She hoped and prayed that the wizard would not come back.

But, alas, the cockerel crowed again, '*Cock-a-doodle-doo! Cock-a-doodle-doo!*' and the evil wizard jumped out from the darkness once more and reached out to grab Amalie.

'You're coming with me!' he said, and just as before the star on Amalie's forehead lit up and the laser beam shot out and knocked him into the next district. This time Amalie noticed the light coming from her forehead.

'What's going on?' she asked.

The star on her forehead answered, 'I am here to protect you but my strength is weakening. I can knock out the wizard seven times only to buy you some time to get away, but after that you're on your own!'

'But where have you come from? What are you?'

'Your mother sent me,' said the star. 'When she saw who your father married after she died she wanted to protect you and make sure you were safe from evil. But hurry, we don't have much time! Get indoors before the wizard comes back. He can only harm you when you are outside at night.'

Amalie listened to what the star told her and she knocked on the door again, even louder than before.

'Stepmother! Stepmother! PLEASE open the door! The evil wizard is coming back to kill me!'

'Can't you hear me?' said the wicked stepmother. 'I don't care if the wizard kills you! In fact, I wish you were dead!'

And as the stepmother spoke the cockerel crowed once more, 'Cock-a-doodle-doo! Cock-a-doodle-doo!' and the evil wizard once again jumped out from the darkness, reaching out to grab Amalie. And for the third time the star on Amalie's forehead lit up and the laser beam shot out and knocked the wizard into the next district. But each time the star hit the wizard it became weaker. Just four more hits and all of its strength would be gone.

Meanwhile, Amalie's father was still away working hard to make money for his family and he knew nothing of his daughter's suffering. But as he worked away his mind drifted and he starting thinking about his first wife. He missed her so very much. That night, when he went back to sleep in his lonely cabin, his first wife came to him in a dream.

'You must go home quickly and look after Amalie!' she said. 'Our daughter needs you. Your new wife has sent an evil wizard to take her away!'

Amalie's father could not believe what he was hearing but he trusted his first wife and loved her very much. He believed that she would only come back from death to tell him something if it was true.

'So what should I do?' said Amalie's father. 'I am far away from Amalie in another country. How can I save her?'

'She has a star of protection on her forehead that is knocking the wizard's strength, but it will only last for a short time. You must wake up and take the first form of transport you see and go back home as fast as you can. When you reach home, run the wizard, your new wife and her children out of town!'

Amalie's father was overwhelmed by everything that he was hearing. Nevertheless he knew the time he had was short and so he got up straight away and did as his first wife told him. There were no planes in those days, so the man had no idea how he was going to get to his home in time to save his daughter. As he stepped out of his cabin the man saw a skinny donkey grazing. His dead wife had told him to take the first form of transport he saw. Surely she could not have meant this skinny donkey? But being an obedient man, Amalie's father approached the donkey and got on its back. At once the donkey took off at great speed!

Back at the house Amalie was outside on her knees. The wizard had continued to try to capture her and the star on her forehead had protected her and knocked him back five times in total.

Amalie cried out to her stepmother, 'Stepmother! Stepmother! I beg you to please open the door! I have only two chances left before the strength in my star runs out. The wizard will destroy me for sure!'

'I don't care!' said the wicked stepmother. 'Now go away and don't disturb me again!' and she went back to sleep.

'*Cock-a-doodle-doo! Cock-a-doodle-doo!*' the cockerel crowed. The wizard jumped out from the darkness and he reached out to grab Amalie for the sixth time. This time only a dim light came from the star on Amalie's forehead and it managed only to push the wizard over a little. The star's strength was waning and Amalie's protection was fading away.

'Ha-ha!' laughed the wizard. 'Is that the best you can do? Now you're all mine!'

And as the wizard grabbed for Amalie for the seventh time, a tiny light flashed from her forehead. The wizard lost his balance, but he shook himself and carried on reaching towards Amalie.

Then suddenly there was a gust of wind – it was Amalie's father on his donkey, just in time to rescue his daughter!

'Get away!' he shouted, and he grabbed hold of the evil wizard with all his strength.

'Let me go!' cried the wizard. 'I'm going to destroy her and you too!'

But Amalie's father did not let him go. Instead, he dragged the evil wizard on to the donkey and they flew to the coast. There, he threw the wizard into the sea and he was never seen again.

And as for the stepmother and stepsisters, Amalie's father went back and woke them all up from their sleep only to throw them out of his house forever. And the old man and his daughter lived happily ever after.

Why Cat Chases Rat

This story is based on a folk tale from Antigua

Once, very long ago, Cat and Rat were the best of friends, or so it seemed. They even lived together in the same house. Cat had allowed Rat to live with him when Rat's house had been flooded. Even when Rat's house had been restored, Rat had never gone back home.

Cat would have done anything for Rat, but the truth was Rat didn't care much for Cat. In front of Cat, Rat was always the perfect gentleman, kind and thoughtful, but behind Cat's back Rat was always saying horrible things – that he smelled bad or that he talked too much or how foolish he was. Cat didn't know this. He thought Rat was his best friend.

That all changed the day Cat's grandfather died. Now Cat was very upset, because he had loved his grandfather very much. Rat pretended that he was sad too, but he didn't care at all. He fussed over Cat, pretending he was trying to make his friend feel better, but behind his back he just rolled his eyes and shook his head, muttering under his breath about how it was a waste of time crying over the dead. Rat was a heartless rodent.

'It is such a sad thing that your grandfather has died,' Rat said to Cat. 'I think you should have a big party to celebrate his life.'

'I'm too sad to think about it,' Cat said.

'Don't you worry about a thing!' Rat said slyly. 'I'll plan the wake for you.'

It was the custom to have a wake when someone died. There would be a church service and people would say good things about them. After the church service, all the animals would come back to the house to show their respect to the family and they would eat and drink and dance. The animals would party all day and often all night. It was the way things were done.

Now Cat felt grateful to have such a thoughtful friend to help him plan his grandfather's wake and he thanked Rat for being so kind.

'No problem,' said Rat, who was already thinking of a way to get something out of it for himself. 'We'll make a big pot of rice for the guests and we'll eat it at your home after the church service. I'll play my fiddle, my tambourine and my triangle at the church service. Don't worry yourself! Just leave it to me.'

Cat was glad he didn't have to think too much about the funeral festivities and he thanked Rat again for being such a good friend.

On the day of the wake, Rat asked Cat to buy a big bag of rice. They put the rice in boiling water to cook on the stove and, when it was ready, they put on their fine suits and set off to the church for the service.

At the church door, Cat greeted all the animals that had come to pay their respects to his grandfather. Rat watched on.

Then suddenly, pretending he had just remembered something, Rat let out a shriek. 'Oh my, oh my!' he said. 'I have forgotten to bring my triangle to play the music at the end of the church service. I'll just go back home and get it!' And with that, Rat rushed off, leaving Cat at the church with the rest of the guests. Once home, Rat immediately went to the big pot of rice and ate a little. It was delicious. Rat then went to the place where he kept his triangle, picked it up and went back to the church.

When Rat arrived back at the church, Mr Frog was saying some nice words about Cat's grandfather at the front of the church for everybody to hear.

'Got it!' Rat said quietly, as he sat down next to Cat. But before Cat could say anything Rat let out a shriek again.

'Oh my, oh my!' he said. 'I have forgotten to bring my tambourine to play the music at the end of the service. I'll just go back home and get it!' And once again Rat rushed off, leaving Cat at the church with the rest of the guests. Once home, Rat immediately went to the big pot of rice and he ate a little more. It was so tasty. Rat then went to the place where he kept his tambourine, picked it up and went back to the church.

When Rat arrived back at the church, Mrs Turtle was saying some nice words about Cat's grandfather at the front of the church for everybody to hear.

'Got it!' Rat said quietly, as he sat down next to Cat. Cat whispered that many people had said such kind words about his grandfather while he had been away, but before Cat could finish speaking Rat let out another shriek. 'Oh my, oh my!' he said. 'I have forgotten to bring my fiddle to play the music at the end of the service. I'll just go back home and get it!' And Rat rushed off again, leaving Cat at the church with the rest of the guests. At home, Rat jumped into the pot to eat the remainder of the rice.

Meanwhile, back at the church, Cat was beginning to think that his friend Rat was acting strangely. He decided to walk ahead of the others and check to see what Rat was up to. When Cat arrived at the house he called out, but there was no reply. Cat saw the fiddle in the cupboard where it was kept and started to worry about what could have happened. He called out again, 'Rat! Rat! Where are you?' Still there was no reply. Then Cat heard a strange *chip chip chip* sound. It was coming from the pot.

'*Chip chip chip chip chip chip.*'

When Cat looked inside the pot he saw all the rice had gone and the greedy Rat, having eaten all the rice, had started to eat the pot too! There he was, chipping away at the empty pot.

'You sneak!' shouted Cat. 'You were coming back here all this time so you could eat up the rice! I'll kill you!'

And Cat reached out to catch Rat.

'Don't kill me! Don't kill me! I beg you, don't kill me!' pleaded Rat.

Now Cat felt sorry for Rat. After all, they had been friends for a long time. So he decided he wouldn't kill him after all. 'All right, all right, I promise I won't kill you.' But Cat was still angry with Rat, and he wanted him to pay.

'You had better run, though,' said Cat, 'because if I catch you your life won't be worth living!' And with that Cat began to chase Rat around his house.

Wherever Rat ran, Cat was hot on his tail. There was no hiding place, even when Rat ran out of the house. Rat ran into the smallest holes, and when Cat could not fit in after him he simply waited patiently until Rat came out again. Rat thought he could outrun Cat but, although he was faster and indeed more nimble, Cat never stopped chasing him.

Eventually Rat grew tired of running. In fact Rat was

exhausted. Unable to run any further, he rolled over, feet in the air, and died.

And Cat had kept his promise. He hadn't killed Rat. And that is why, to this day, you will always see Cat chasing Rat around and around and around.

As for Cat's grandfather's wake, everyone felt sorry for Cat after seeing how Rat had eaten all the rice, and each of the guests decided to go home and pick up some food to take to Cat's house. So there was plenty to eat at the wake – and greedy Rat missed out on a feast!

Why Rabbit has a Short Tail

This story is based on a folk tale from Antigua

It was a particularly hot summer and Rabbit was feeling so warm he thought he would melt. Rabbit complained to everyone he met about how hot he was. Now this was back in the days when Rabbit's tail was long and bushy. Barracuda heard Rabbit moaning about the heat and decided he would trick Rabbit.

He watched Rabbit from the water for some time and then he called, 'Rabbit! I can see you are hot. I can help. I can tell you how to get cool!'

Rabbit wasn't interested in anything Barracuda had to say, as he was sure the huge fish was trying to trick him and eat him up.

'It's all right, Barracuda, I'm fine!' Rabbit called back.

But Rabbit wasn't fine. The fur on his back was much too thick and heavy for the heat, and he was feeling terrible.

'I know what you're thinking!' said Barracuda. 'You think I want to eat you. That's not true. I only want to help a brother out. It's mighty cool in this water,' and Barracuda started to show off about how cool the water was by swimming around.

Still Rabbit didn't fall for his trick. 'I am not coming into that water, Barracuda!' said Rabbit. 'If I get in there, you're going to eat me for sure.'

Well, they went on like that for some time, with Barracuda telling Rabbit how cool the water was, and Rabbit telling Barracuda that he wasn't going to get in. Eventually Barracuda decided to try another way.

'You don't need to get into the water,' he said. 'Just dip the tip of your tail in, and when the water cools your tail down it will send the coolness up to the rest of your body. Then you will not be so hot.'

Rabbit thought about what Barracuda had said. Perhaps if he put just the tip of his tail in the water, that would cool him down and he would still be safe.

'Very well,' said Rabbit, 'I will just put the tip of my tail in the water. But you must move far away from the edge so I am sure to be safe!'

'Very well,' said Barracuda, and he swam further away from the edge so that Rabbit felt safe.

So Rabbit came to the edge of the water while Barracuda looked on, waiting for his moment to pounce. When Rabbit had put the tip of his tail in the water Barracuda said, 'How does that feel, Rabbit?'

Rabbit was enjoying the little bit of coolness that the tip of his tail was feeling, but the rest of his body was still hot.

'The tip of my tail is cool,' he said, 'but the rest of me is still hot.'

'That's strange,' said Barracuda. 'It's common knowledge that if you put the tip of your tail in cool water the coolness from the water shoots up the tail to the rest of the body and cools you down. Maybe you need to put a little more of your tail in the water for you to feel the benefit.'

Rabbit wasn't sure if this was a good idea. Nevertheless, he was so hot he thought he would try it. After all, it wasn't as if he was putting his whole body in the water. It was just his tail.

Rabbit leaned back a little, so that more of his tail could get deeper into the water.

'Any better?' asked Barracuda.

'Not really,' said Rabbit.

'Then put a little bit more of your tail in the water,' said Barracuda.

Rabbit thought about it. He knew Barracuda was up to something and he was determined not to get caught out.

'I will put more of my tail in the water, but you must move even further away from the edge so I am sure to be safe!'

'Very well,' said Barracuda, and he swam further away from the edge so that Rabbit felt safe.

Once he had done this, Rabbit edged back a little bit more until the whole of his tail was in the water.

It felt so cool when he swished his long bushy tail in the water. As he did so, he was able to splash some of the cool water on to his hot furry back.

'This feels much better,' Rabbit said, enjoying the splashes on his body.

As Rabbit got carried away with splashing his tail in the water, Barracuda began to inch closer and closer. Rabbit, so engrossed in sprinkling water on his back, didn't even notice until it was too late! Barracuda opened his big mouth and bit off most of Rabbit's tail. Rabbit pulled himself away immediately so that he wasn't eaten all up, but that is why, to this day, Rabbit has a short tail.

TALES FROM

THE
CARIBBEAN

With Puffin Classics, the adventure isn't
over when you reach the final page.
Want to discover more about the people
and places that inspired these stories?
Read on . . .

CONTENTS

The Caribbean is an area of the Atlantic Ocean. On the west, the sea is bounded by the United States, Central and South America. On the east, there is a string of islands stretching for about 2,000 miles, known as the West Indies. Some islands are made of limestone or coral – but most are volcanic. Some of the volcanoes are still active!

The islands have a tropical climate, and the warm weather and good rainfall, together with rich soil, means that plants grow very well. Originally the islands were inhabited by the Taino and Carib peoples. However, when European explorers arrived, many of the indigenous people died resisting the invasion. The Europeans also brought diseases such as smallpox. The island dwellers had no defence against such illnesses, and enormous numbers died.

Some of the European explorers – most of them were British, Dutch, French, Portuguese and Spanish – decided to take over the islands, so they could benefit from farming them. Crops like sugar and tobacco were very profitable, but needed a great many labourers to work the land. For many years, they brought shiploads of black people from West Africa to work as slaves. The masters grew rich, but the slaves were treated badly and they got no payment for their labour.

Britain abolished slavery in the countries it ruled in 1807, and other countries eventually did the same. The black slave Toussaint l'Ouverture started as a leader of a slave rebellion, fighting Spain and France, and ended as Governor-General of Saint-Domingue (now Haiti). These days, the islands of the West Indies are independent, though some still have connections with the European nations who used to rule them.

Today, the majority of West Indians are descended from black Africans. There are also people of European descent – and some come from Asia! After slavery was abolished, Chinese and East Indian farm workers came to the West Indies, looking for work . . . and all these different people brought stories from their own countries, and told them in their own languages. So as well as Carib stories (there are a very few Caribs living in remote parts of Dominica), there are stories told in Spanish in Cuba, the Dominican Republic and Puerto Rico, Dutch stories in Aruba and the Dutch Antilles, French stories in Haiti, Guadeloupe and Martinique, and English stories in most of the other islands. And that doesn't include the African stories and the languages they were told in!

All over the world, people tell stories. Some of these stories are very old, and were enjoyed long before tales were written down. They tell of such things as how the people thought the world was made, or of how good people or poor people did well.

One of the most popular characters in these stories is the trickster. Tricksters are usually clever. They use their brains and not their strength. They can bring gifts or messages from the gods, or cause terrible trouble. They can be heroes – or villains. They can be nasty and greedy, or friendly and helpful. They don't obey the rules. You just can't tell with a trickster. And they always survive. Even the most dreadful punishments or accidents don't squash them.

Very often the trickster is an animal – Reynard the Fox in France, or Coyote amongst some Native American peoples. In China there's a very tricky monkey king, Sun Wukong. Just occasionally it's a human – Till Eulenspiegel in Germany, or Prometheus in ancient Greek stories, who steals fire from the gods to give to human beings – and Robin Hood in England is a trickster!

In these stories from the Caribbean, we meet two of the world's most famous tricksters, Brer Rabbit and Anansi the spider-man. Both of them come originally from Africa!

Brer Rabbit (he's called Compère Lapin in French-speaking parts of the Caribbean) was a hare in Africa. Many stories about him come from the Bantu people of Central and South

Africa. However, when black people arrived in the New World, the hare became a rabbit. In the United States, the stories were collected by Joel Chandler Harris, who introduced them to a wide audience through 'Uncle Remus', an old black story-teller.

Anansi came originally from the Ashanti people of Ghana. He's always a spider, but he often looks like a man. Anansi has special skills and wisdom in speech, and is the spirit who knows all stories – once they belonged to the Sky God, but Anansi tricked his way into getting every one of them.

Black people taken to the West Indies and to northern America as slaves told each other the stories they remembered from home, adapting them to their new surroundings. They enjoyed the fact that Brer Rabbit or Anansi – small, weak creatures – often tricked the rulers and masters!

The West Indies – the name for all the islands of the Caribbean together – are warm, well-watered, and mostly very fertile (though hurricanes and tropical storms can do a great deal of damage!).

Palm trees provide West Indians with bananas and coconuts, and a huge variety of other plants that provide food are grown – from tomatoes, citrus fruits and coffee to more exotic things such as breadfruit, soursops, cassava and plantains. With seas full of fish – including bonitos and tuna, and shellfish like clams and crabs – and livestock such as pigs and chickens, cooks have plenty of interesting materials to use.

Over the years people from many parts of the world have come to the Caribbean, so there are recipes of all kinds in use. Some, like johnnycake (which, in its original form, was a flat bread made by cooking a sort of maize porridge) or grated and fried cassava – this is poisonous if it isn't properly prepared – go back to the bad days of slavery when many people had to live on very little. Some have become well-known around the world – rice and peas, for example, which is found everywhere in the Caribbean (although the dish is called rice and peas, the recipe is made up of rice and red beans, along with coconut cream, herbs and spices), or jerk chicken which is a very smoky, spicy barbecued chicken that takes several hours to prepare.

One of the essential ingredients for jerk chicken – and for many other savoury dishes – is the Scotch Bonnet chilli pepper. This is a very hot pepper indeed (in Guyana, in South America, it's called the 'ball-of-fire' pepper). As well as chillis, West Indians like many other spices to flavour their food. Even cakes and ice creams may have ginger or black pepper in them!

Another ingredient in many dishes is rum. This is an alcoholic spirit, made from sugar. And it isn't just a drink. Like chillis and other spices, it appears in all sorts of dishes. It can even be used to make jerk chicken!

The Caribbean has a hot climate, and hot, spicy food. What could be better with these than a long, cool drink . . .?

Even if summer is cold and wet, this will inspire you to dream of lovely hot summer days – think of being on a tropical island, with the sea lapping the beach . . .

You will need:

- 1 ¼ pt/ 581 ml / 2 ½ cups of orange juice
- ⅝ pt/ 298 ml / 1 ¼ cups pineapple juice
- ⅛ pt / 60 ml / ¼ cup of lime juice
- 2 tbls grenadine

What you do:

Pour all the juice into a big jug, and stir well. Put the mixture into the fridge, and chill for several hours. Pour into glasses – there should be enough here for four – and pour 1 ½ teaspoons of grenadine down the inside of each glass.

Enjoy!

Track down a trickster! Can you track down some other trickster stories? What part of the world do they come from, and what sort of a character is the trickster? If you were going to invent a tricky character, what sort would you have?

Get a globe or an atlas. Can you find all the Caribbean islands mentioned in the stories? Can you find West Africa too? If you went to a strange country, far away from your home, which stories would you like to tell people?

How may words of three letters or more can you make from the letters in the word CARIBBEAN? We found 71. Can you beat us?

SLAVERY

Slavery is a system which allows one person to own another. The slave is property, and can be bought and sold. The children of slaves (also slaves) can be sold to owners far away from their parents. A slave is not paid, but must work at whatever the master orders, however hard or difficult the work is. There are no regulations about the hours a slave can work, and no breaks or holidays. The master should provide shelter, clothes and food, but may not, or only provide very poor ones.

Slavery probably started early in prehistoric times, when prisoners taken in war were made to work on farms. Other slaves were probably criminals, or people who had got into debt.

Every society of the ancient world – China, India, Egypt, the Middle East – used slaves. In ancient Greece and in the Roman Empire, there were huge numbers of slaves. They did most of the work.

After the Roman Empire broke up, there wasn't a need for slaves in many parts of Europe. Instead, many people were tied to the land. They were serfs, and could not move about or do very much without their lord's permission. However, the old style of slavery still existed around the Mediterranean and down into Africa.

From the beginning of the fifteenth century, Europeans started to investigate the world around them. They sailed down the coast of Africa, eventually reaching India by sea. They sailed across the Atlantic, in time setting up colonies in the West Indies and in the Americas.

The most profitable crop to grow was sugar, but coffee, cotton, and tobacco were in great demand in Europe. The farms, called plantations, were often very big, and needed a great number of people to work on them. There were chieftains in West Africa who were happy to sell prisoners of war and members of other tribes to slave traders, who loaded their ships full and sailed across the ocean to the slave markets, where the cargoes were sold on. This became known as 'the Triangle Trade' – a ship from Britain, say, would sail to West Africa, fill up with slaves, sail to (for example) Jamaica, sell the slaves, fill the ship with sugar or some other profitable crop, then head back to Britain to make further money selling this cargo.

As time went by, more and more people began to think it was a terrible thing to treat human beings as slaves. They had to fight hard against slavery, because the slave trade made so much money, but Parliament abolished slavery in Britain in 1807, and Congress in the United Sates forbade the import of African slaves in 1808 (though the slaves already there were not freed until some time later). France freed all its remaining slaves in 1848.

But slavery continued in many parts of the world. Today, it is against the law in most countries – but sadly, it still exists. No one really knows how many people are enslaved, and it seems that some governments might not be powerful enough to stop it even if they wanted to.

barracuda – a large, fierce tropical fish

breadfruit – the round, starchy fruit of an evergreen tree belonging to the mulberry family which can be eaten as a vegetable or used to make a sort of flour

Brer – dialect way of saying brother

callaloo – a plant with leaves that can be cooked and eaten as a green vegetable, or a stew or soup made from the leaves

Carib – a people who lived in the northern part of South America and who also settled on some West Indian islands. It is also the name of their language

cassava – the starchy root of several shrubs of the spurge family: the root can be roasted and eaten as bread

christophine – a pear-shaped fruit that grows on a vine, related to melons, squashes and cucumbers

Compère – part of the French name for Brer Rabbit – it means 'godfather'

coupay cord-la – dialect for 'cut the rope' or 'cut the string'

Creole – someone of European – usually French or Spanish – descent, born in the West Indies. It is also the name of the French or Spanish dialect such a person may speak

hammock – a kind of bed made from a strip of canvas or rope mesh tied to a support at each end

indigenous – something that grows or lives or occurs naturally in a particular place

jalousie – the Kwéyòl word to describe a jealous person; it is also the word used for a window blind with horizontal slats that can be adjusted to let in air and light

johnnycake – West Indian johnnycakes are a kind of fried bread made from flour, butter, sugar, salt and water

Kwéyòl – a language spoken which has its origins in French and African languages

maman – French for mum or mummy

mapou tree – the silk-cotton tree, venerated by many in Haiti

okra – a plant belonging to the mallow family. Its long green pods are eaten as a vegetable, especially in soups and stews

passion fruit – the edible purple fruit of the passion flower, an evergreen climbing plant

patois – the dialect of a particular area, usually considered rough and uneducated

pepper bush – the plant on which the Scotch Bonnet chilli grows

plantain – a kind of banana, starchy and not very sweet when green. It is used as a vegetable. The plantain can be cooked when it is yellow too, and then it tastes sweet

plateau – an area of flat high ground

Port-au-Prince – the capital city of Haiti

raconteur – a story-teller

savannah – in tropical areas, a grassy plain with few trees

Sookooyah – a mythical scary spirit said to be seen flying about at night like a ball of fire on some Caribbean islands, including Dominica

soursop – a small evergreen tree of the custard apple family, and its large, white, slightly acid fruit

souse – a Caribbean broth dish made from spicy picked pork. Although there are various types of Caribbean souse (such as beef and chicken), pork is the most common

sweet potato – the edible tuberous root of a tropical vine. It is sometimes called a yam, but the two plants are different

yam – the edible tuberous root of a tropical vine

If you have enjoyed *Tales from the Caribbean* you may
like to read more short stories and legends:

Tales from Africa by K. P. Kojo
Tales from India by Bali Rai

Available in Puffin Classics